"WHAT SHI

"I said I love you. I you and I guess I sh yet, but you're all I can think about."

It did seem sudden to Cassie. Too sudden. She had to know.

"Do you love me because of my money?"

A little chuckle escaped from his lips before he answered, "I love you in spite of it." Then Luke waited quietly as the waves tumbled and a gull called overhead. When Cassie just stood there looking stunned, he added, "I hadn't planned to tell you like this. I wanted moonlight in a garden of roses with an orchestra playing in the background. But roses are out of season and orchestras cost a bundle."

"I hear there'll be moonlight tonight," she said, finding her tongue at last. "One out of three isn't bad."

Dear Reader:

SILHOUETTE DESIRE is an exciting new line of contemporary romances from Silhouette Books. During the past year, many Silhouette readers have written in telling us what other types of stories they'd like to read from Silhouette, and we've kept these comments and suggestions in mind in developing SILHOUETTE DESIRE.

DESIREs feature all of the elements you like to see in a romance, plus a more sensual, provocative story. So if you want to experience all the excitement, passion and joy of falling in love, then SILHOUETTE DESIRE is for you.

For more details write to:

Jane Nicholls
Silhouette Books
PO Box 236
Thornton Road
Croydon
Surrey CR9 3RU

LYNDA TRENT
Simple Pleasures

Silhouette Desire
Originally Published by Silhouette Books
division of
Harlequin Enterprises Ltd.

First published in Great Britain 1986
by Silhouette Books, 15–16 Brook's Mews, London W1A 1DR

ISBN 0 373 05223 5

22–0186

Made and printed in Great Britain by
Richard Clay (The Chaucer Press) Ltd,
Bungay, Suffolk

LYNDA TRENT
started writing at the insistence of a friend, but it was her husband who provided moral support whenever her resolve flagged. Now, as she puts it, "Both he and I are full-time writers and love it."

Another Silhouette Book by Lynda Trent

Silhouette Desire

The Enchantment

For further information about Silhouette Books please write to:

Jane Nicholls
Silhouette Books
PO Box 236
Thornton Road
Croydon
Surrey CR9 3RU

To Zelrna and Andrew Goodlett
for being there

1

Cassie knew it was going to be a bad day when the fish died. Not that she was all that fond of Mr. Beebles, but her nephew had bought it for her with his own allowance, and Mr. Beebles had chosen to depart on the morning when Cassie was already late for work.

She gazed down at the goldfish and sighed. Not wanting to come home to a dead fish, Cassie took the bowl to the bathroom and grimaced as she gave the late Mr. Beebles an appropriate burial at sea. She wrinkled her freckled nose and wondered how anything that lived in what amounted to a perpetual bath could smell so bad. She rinsed the bowl and left it on the counter top. With any luck at all she could find a Beebles ringer at the pet shop and her nephew would never know the difference.

Grabbing the spaghetti strap of her leather purse as

she passed through the bedroom, Cassie glanced at her alarm clock. Eight-thirty! She should be in the flower shop now. With a groan, she raced through the house and out to the garage. Although her intentions were always good—or so she thought—punctuality had never been her strong suit.

A breeze laden with the scents of autumn and sea air lifted her sable brown bangs and ruffled her shoulder-length hair. Automatically Cassie pushed a thick strand behind her ear, just as her mother had told her not to do for the past twenty-four years.

She wrestled open the door of her aging car and managed to slam it shut behind her on the second try. Soon the latch would give out altogether, she mused gloomily, and she would have to hold it closed with one hand and drive with the other. Assuming the car would start. The engine wheezed in objection but finally choked into life. Not wanting to overtax the moody transmission, Cassie let gravity roll the car out of the garage and into the street, then eased the gearshift into first position.

"At least you're paid for," Cassie consoled the worn-out car. "You don't cost me anything each month." The same couldn't be said of her telephone, unfortunately. She had an overdue notice in her purse. And the chances of Elwin Glass giving her a raise were about zero—especially with her being late again this week.

"At least this is Saturday," Cassie said to the rattling engine as she stopped for a traffic light. "By noon I'll be through for the weekend."

The man standing on the corner looked at her

curiously, and Cassie blushed when she realized she had spoken aloud. Hastily she rolled up her window and waited impatiently for the light to change.

When it was her turn to go, she sped down the streets of Plymouth, pushing the speed limit and watching for patrol cars. The last thing she needed with her finances in such bruised shape was another speeding ticket.

Her chocolate brown eyes flicked over the cars in the tiny parking lot behind the row of buildings that housed the flower shop. No Mustang. That meant her boss was also late and she had a chance of getting in unnoticed.

The car had barely rolled to a stop before Cassie leaped out, heaved the door shut, and promptly tripped over the parking curb. Fortunately, she landed on her palms, breaking her fall. She carefully sat up and surveyed herself: palms red but not bleeding, shoes scuffed, panty hose miraculously not snagged, contents of purse strewn over the sidewalk. Cassie muttered an expletive that would have shocked her mother and began shoveling the odds and ends back into her purse—four tubes of lipstick, a hairbrush, several credit cards, the overdue phone bill, and the green and gold stub of a lottery ticket. She snorted derisively. With luck like hers she should have saved the two dollars she paid for the ticket and put the money toward her phone bill. That was what she got for listening to her sister, Trina. Cassie had never before bought a lottery ticket until this month, the month she had run short of money.

Scrambling to her feet, Cassie brushed the dust

from her clothing while she looked about to see if anyone had seen her fall. Thankful that her embarrassment was not compounded by witnesses, Cassie hurriedly unlocked the back door of the florist shop and stepped into the scented darkness, breathing a sigh of relief. The intermingling fragrances of the carnations and roses on the cool air greeted her in the same welcoming way they did every morning. She filled her lungs with the sweetness and smiled. Before the shop was opened for the day, it had a magical sense, as if it were a tiny forest of flowers and ferns.

Cassie flipped on the fluorescent lights and again inhaled the perfumed air. She loved working with flowers, and she knew she had a talent for arrangements. Elwin Glass was a scrooge for not paying her a decent salary, she noted not for the first time; then she set the thought aside. She knew she could make more money working elsewhere, but she enjoyed her job and she wasn't going to change. Somehow she would manage. She always did.

As she passed through the work area to the showroom, she made mental notes of the things that needed to be done that morning, then unlocked the front door and flipped over the Open sign. A quick survey of the flowers on display told her it was time to water, so she slipped on the red apron with "Daisy Dilly Flower Shoppe" spelled out in yellow posies. Although she thought the apron's design and color scheme could be improved, the wet-look plastic fabric had saved her clothes from stains on more than one occasion.

After pushing up the elbows of her blue and white

pinstripe blouse, Cassie filled the bright red watering can.

The phone rang, and she balanced the receiver between ear and shoulder as she stretched to water the row of Swedish ivies. "Daisy Dilly. May I help you? Oh, hi, Penny. Sure, I can fill in for you Tuesday night. Big date?"

Cassie expertly caught the overflow from the pot as she overwatered one of the ivies. "No, Penny, you know I don't mind. Have fun. Bye." Penny had a new boyfriend, and Cassie often covered for her at the crisis hot line where they both did volunteer work. Cassie's regular night was Thursday, but she was there in Penny's stead on Tuesdays almost as often.

She turned the group of potted begonias and Chinese forget-me-nots so their other sides could bask in the sunlight from the window. In a rare pensive mood, Cassie snapped off the few dead blooms. When she looked at her life as a whole, she felt it had little more excitement in it than these plants. Her days and nights fit a regulated pattern that she found restricted when she stopped to think about it, which was seldom because she was basically a happy person. Given her choice, she would have picked a more glamorous life with travel and paid-up phone bills, but Cassie had the knack of seeing an entire universe in a single raindrop, and she rarely paid heed to her sister's often-repeated opinion that her life was dull, if not boring.

The bell jingled over the front door, and she went into the showroom. "May I help you?" she asked the couple who had entered.

"Maybe." The short man scowled up at his rather large wife, then glared back at Cassie. Producing a small pink card, he demanded, "Do you know anything about this?"

Cassie looked from the man to his embarrassed wife as she took the card. The Daisy Dilly logo was in one corner, and her own handwriting said, "Don't go away mad. Let's give it another try. Luke."

"Yes, I remember. This order came in the day before yesterday." She smiled at the man, who continued to frown.

"Who's Luke!" he demanded.

Cassie's smile faltered. "I have no idea."

"Please, Harvey," the woman spoke up. "Let's just go. Okay? It was some sort of mix-up."

He ignored her. "Are you the one who handled this order?" he asked Cassie.

"Yes, but . . ."

"Well, who placed it?"

"I . . . I have no idea. The order was phoned." She was growing irritated at the man's attitude.

"Harvey, please!" the woman begged. "I told you I don't know anybody named Luke." She timidly touched his coat sleeve.

Harvey brushed off her imploring fingers. "We've been over that, Ethel!" To Cassie he said, "We were about to leave on a cruise—one of those love-boat deals, a second honeymoon—when we go to our cabin, and what do I find? This!" He gestured angrily with the card.

"There must have been some mistake," Cassie said

carefully. A bon-voyage bouquet had been sent. Surely she hadn't . . .

"I'll say there was a mistake!" Harvey glared at his luckless wife, who was a good head taller and twenty pounds heavier than he was. "I can't trust you out of my sight!"

"This is so embarrassing," the woman moaned to Cassie. Turning back to her husband, she said, "I told you over and over. I don't know anybody named Luke."

"That's even worse! Lying yet! Let's go, Ethel!"

Cassie shook her head in wonder as Harvey strode away, leaving Ethel to hurry after him. She had never seen such a display of misplaced jealousy; the woman hardly fit the image of a *femme fatale*. Cassie bit her lower lip nervously. That could only mean one thing—two orders must have been mixed up. She doubted Elwin had ever made such an error, and that left only one culprit. Herself.

Through the front window of the shop, Cassie watched as Harvey almost ran into a tall man carrying a handful of flowers. They exchanged curt apologies, and the second man turned toward the door of the flower shop. Cassie backed deeper into the rows of plants as he shouldered open the door. "May I help you?" she asked with growing trepidation. The bedraggled flowers clutched tightly in his fist looked all too familiar.

"I want to speak to the person in charge here," he said in no-nonsense tones, his words softened slightly by his Southern accent.

"That's me—I—me," she corrected hastily. He was tall and broad shouldered and he moved with the natural grace of an athlete. He wore a heather brown sweater in a muted Argyle pattern, and dark brown slacks that hugged his lean waist and hips. The wind had ruffled his dark red-brown hair, giving him an even more sensuous air. His eyes, glinting with suppressed emotion, were the deep velvety green of pine needles. Although his body seemed to snap with restrained anger, Cassie couldn't help noticing how handsome he was. His nose was straight and aristocratic and his forehead broad and high, giving him a look of keen intelligence. A tiny cleft dinted his square chin, and his jawbones flared slightly, suggesting a German ancestry.

Feeling discretion was in order, Cassie sidestepped so that the counter was between her and the obviously upset man. "I'm in charge," she said in what she hoped was a competent tone.

He slapped the bouquet down on the counter and braced himself on his square palms, leaning toward her. A wrinkled banner reading "Bon Voyage" was tangled among the flowers' leaves and trailed accusingly over the Formica counter top. "Do you have any explanation as to why you sent my girlfriend these flowers instead of the ones I ordered?" His deep voice was a barely controlled growl.

"You're Luke!" Cassie exclaimed as she put the pieces together.

"Do we know each other?" he asked, somewhat distracted by her unexpected use of his name.

Cassie moved back a step. "No, we've never met."

He paused as if trying to make sense of this, then demanded, "Well? Can you explain why you sent *this* to 504 Elm Street, instead of the roses I ordered?" Again he swatted the counter with the flowers.

"There was a mix-up," she ventured. Was he dangerous? Those flowers looked as if he had whacked them against telephone poles for blocks. "I—"

"A mix-up! I ordered two dozen red roses as a peace offering, and you sent a bon-voyage arrangement? Maureen says she's never going to speak to me again!"

"Don't you yell at me like that!" Cassie said, her anger leaping to meet his. "People make mistakes, you know! This really isn't my day! First Mr. Beebles died and then I nearly couldn't get the car started and that made me even later to work and I fell in the parking lot! And you think *you* have problems? I can tell you about problems! Those flowers were a stupid mix-up and I apologize! Now, I don't want to hear another word about them!" She had rounded the counter and was glaring up at him with fire glinting in her eyes.

After a long hesitation, he grabbed the flowers, turned on his heel and stalked out. Cassie edged to the window and watched as he tossed the flowers in a garbage can, ran his long fingers through his thick reddish brown hair and seemed to be drawing a steadying breath. Then he turned and purposefully strode back toward the flower shop.

Cassie scurried to a position of dubious safety behind the counter just as he came through the door. He crossed the shop and studied her for a moment before he said, "Let's try it again. I'm Luke Bennett."

"Cassie Collins," she said automatically, then cursed herself silently for her stupidity. Now this maniac knew her name.

"Did you hurt yourself?"

"What?" she gasped.

"You said you fell in the parking lot. Are you okay?"

"I'm all right," she hedged.

"This Mr. Beebles who died. Was he a friend or a relative?" he asked with a note of true concern.

"He was a fish." She couldn't decide if she should pick up a vase to use as a weapon, or just take her chances running.

Luke nodded as if what she'd said made perfect sense. "Now," he went on. "I had a fight with my girlfriend. It was only one of many, but this time she was more upset than usual so I sent her flowers to apologize."

"I know. And I'm really so sorry," Cassie commiserated. "Your flowers went to the wrong person. That was the couple who just left. He wouldn't listen to me or his wife, and he's sure she's running around with you, and he wouldn't let me explain, and he wouldn't listen to her. Your girlfriend must have been terribly upset! Give me her name and number and I'll call and explain. I could send her more flowers, but they'll come out of my paycheck and I can't afford to pay my telephone bill as it is. I—"

"Hold it!" He made a calming motion with his

outstretched hands. "Maybe I ought to go out again and try one more time."

Cassie caught her lower lip in her teeth. Whenever she was upset she always tended to let her tongue run away with her words. "I'm sorry," she said contritely. "I guess I got carried away again. I suppose you'll want to speak to my boss, Elwin Glass. What I did was really inexcusable. Did you like her very much? Your girlfriend, I mean."

"Enough to try to make up with her. Not enough to be heartbroken that she won't speak to me. She didn't believe me when I tried to tell her it was a mistake that she got the bon-voyage bouquet." He gave her a sideways glance. "You can't pay your phone bill?"

"I didn't mean to tell you that. Forget I mentioned it. Give me her address and I'll send over the roses you ordered." She found a pencil and an order blank and waited expectantly.

"On the card put, 'Cassie, Thanks for having lunch with me,' and send it to your home address."

"To me?" she asked in confusion. "But I never had lunch with you."

"I know, but I'm getting ready to ask you if you will."

"You can't do that! I wrecked your relationship with your girlfriend."

"I know. Having lunch with me is the least you can do to repay me."

Suddenly Cassie smiled, and a dimple appeared in one cheek. "All right. It's a deal," she surprised herself by saying.

"When is your lunch hour?"

"I get off at noon today. Where should I meet you?" She knew she shouldn't agree to this. Her friends were always telling her she was much too impulsive.

"I'll pick you up here. Do you like Italian food?"

"Sure." What harm could it do to have lunch with him? He'd had every right to be angry, and he could have even cost her her job if he had taken his complaint to Elwin.

Luke smiled, and she felt a warmth steal over her. "Great," he said as casually as if they had not just been at each other's throats. "See you at noon."

Cassie watched Luke leave the shop, and she moved quickly to the window to see him stroll down the street. He looked every bit as good from the back as he did from the front. Perhaps, she decided, the day wasn't such a disaster after all.

All morning Cassie's mood swung between excitement over seeing Luke again and worry that she had agreed to go out with a perfect stranger. For all she knew he could be an ax murderer or a demented pervert. Still, she mused as the clock passed eleven-thirty, his eyes weren't weird. They were a deep green that reminded her of lazy summers and cool shade. She had always maintained she could tell anyone's personality by his eyes, and if that was true, she could trust Luke completely. However, by the time she took off her red plastic apron and was preparing to lock up the store, her mood had made another drastic swing and she was questioning the sanity of ever agreeing to go out with him. After all, he had been pretty rough on that bunch of flowers. Maybe he was bad tempered. Reluctantly, Cassie decided to tell him when he showed up that she had changed her mind.

Noon came and passed, but Luke didn't walk through the door. For someone who was never on time herself, this irritated Cassie unreasonably. Sure, she had decided not to go, but he didn't know that. Who did he think he was, standing her up?

At twelve-thirty she could find no more excuses to wait for him, so she locked up, shouldered her bag and went out the back.

Luke stood in the parking lot leaning patiently against the fender of a pale blue Audi. When he saw her, he straightened with a smile.

Cassie paused as her emotions gave an unexpected lurch. He was more handsome than she remembered—and taller. In the sunlight, his hair had fiery highlights and his eyes were the clear green of river moss. Within a breath she forgot her decision not to see him.

"I'm sorry I'm late," she said as she neared him. "When you didn't come in, I thought you had changed your mind." That was all wrong, she chastised herself. Now he would think she was accustomed to being stood up on dates.

"I wasn't sure whether you would get off on time or if your boss would object to my coming in to get you. There's a half-hour parking limit out front, so I came back here instead."

Cassie paused and let her eyes sweep from him to the spotlessly clean Audi, then to her own car parked beside it. The contrast was striking. As he set her heart to fluttering with a slow grin, she commented, "You don't look like the sort of person that goes around picking people up in flower shops."

His grin broadened. "What sort of person usually picks up women in your shop?"

Cassie had the grace to blush. "I don't know. You're the first one." To cover her embarrassment she blurted out, "What do you do for a living?"

"When I'm not beating flowers or leching after women, you mean? I work for Pan-Ways Corporation."

"That big plant outside of town? What do you do there?"

"I'm an engineer. I'm working on a space suit design."

"Space suit? In Plymouth, Massachusetts? I thought they were made in Houston or maybe Washington."

"No, we have a contract to design a prototype, as do several other companies. They're all submitted to NASA, and whichever company has the best idea gets a contract to manufacture the astronauts' suits."

"How interesting! Do you know any astronauts?"

"A few. Sally Ride was up here last week."

Cassie couldn't think how to respond. To her, the astronauts had the untouchable glamour of old-time movie stars. Yet Luke sounded as if they were merely casual acquaintances. "Space suits! I never thought about anyone designing them. I guess I must have assumed they were built automatically."

Luke smiled and gestured at the parking lot. "I thought you might want to take your car home. I can follow you, and then we'll go to lunch in my car."

Cassie glanced surreptitiously from her battered heap to the Audi and back again. No, she just couldn't do it. With a shrug and a smile, she said, "I took a cab in today." She felt marginally guilty over her lie, but she just couldn't admit to being the owner of the rolling wreck.

Luke walked her to the passenger side and opened the door. "I'm glad you agreed to go out with me. By the way, I don't make a habit of asking strangers out, either."

She squinted against the sun to look up at him. "Then why did you?"

"Because I want to get to know you."

Luke shut her door, and she watched him walk around the car. Had he meant the words to sound so intimate? With his Southern accent, everything he said had the quality of a caress about it.

They drove back toward the heart of town. Cassie, who could usually talk to anyone about anything, found herself as tongue-tied as a teenager on her first date. Luke, too, was quiet. After a while Cassie relaxed and made a few casual comments about the weather, all of which sounded stilted and dull to her own ears. Talk! she silently commanded herself. Talk, or you'll never see him again! This was enough to drive all conversation from her brain, and she sat miserably silent.

He parked on a narrow side street and she looked around. "Where's the restaurant? This looks like a residential section."

"Down this alley."

He took her arm and led her down a tree-lined lane.

Cassie glanced at him suspiciously. She had lived in Plymouth all her life and she knew of no restaurant in this area. The bordering fences were low and the yards close together. If he made any overt moves, she figured she could elbow him in the solar plexus, jump the fence, and run away before he could catch her.

As she was finishing the development of her defense strategy, Luke opened a low gate and they entered a hedge-rimmed yard. A flagstone walk led to what had once been a carriage house but now bore a discreet sign that read "Luigi and Sal's."

"There really is a restaurant!" she exclaimed.

"Of course. Did you think I was abducting you?"

"Of course not!" she answered quickly.

Luke opened the wooden door and had to duck his head under the low lintel. Inside, the atmosphere was one of jovial friendliness. Cassie followed a waitress to a booth and slid into the dimly lit interior.

"How did you ever find this place? I had no idea it was here."

"Sal and Luigi are friends of mine. They don't advertise. They say word of mouth is more effective. They must be right, because sometimes it's so crowded you can't get a table for an hour."

After they ordered and the waitress had gone, Luke said, "Tell me about yourself. Have you lived here long?"

"Goodness yes. In Plymouth you're counted as a newcomer unless your family has been here at least three generations." She still felt a little silly for her earlier doubts of him.

"And yours has been here that long?"

"Would you believe the *Mayflower?*"

"The *Mayflower?* Now I know you're pulling my leg."

"No, I'm serious. Both my mother and my sister belong to the DAR."

"That's the Daughters of the American Revolution, isn't it? Aren't you a member?"

"No, I'm not much on clubs. If I were, I'd probably have joined a group to save the wild horses or something like that."

"I gather your family still lives here, too?"

"Yes. Mom is a widow, and I have an older sister named Trina, who's married and has a son."

Their meal arrived, and Cassie tasted her lasagna appreciatively. "Terrific! Have you lived in Plymouth long?"

"Three years. I'm from North Carolina, but I'm a willing transplant."

Cassie smiled. "I've been trying to place your accent." Every time he had spoken, she had felt a tingle run through her. Southern accents weren't very common in Massachusetts.

"You mentioned a mother and a sister. Is there a man in your life as well?"

After a pause, Cassie said, "No. Not anymore." That reminded her of their meeting, and she said, "Luke, please give me your girlfriend's name. I want to try to straighten out the mess I caused. You're being terribly nice about it, but I want to make amends between you." She faltered. That wasn't at all what she wanted.

"Take my word for it, there's no need. Maureen and

I have dated most of the past year. During that time she's said good-bye forever at least a dozen times."

"So she will forgive you?" Cassie felt her heart plummet.

"Probably. This time, however, I may not want her to." He gazed across the table at Cassie. "Not if there's a chance you'll see me again."

"Me? You don't even know me." Cassie studied his face for any sign of teasing. He seemed to be serious.

"I want to get to know you."

"What if you do and you don't like me?"

"I don't think there's the slightest chance of that." His voice had softened to a husky intonation that made her entire body aware of his.

"Even my friends say I'm a little wacky," she warned breathlessly. "I've been told I could try the patience of a saint."

He smiled again. "I'm no saint."

She had no answer for that. "Then I guess it's okay if you get to know me."

Luke pushed aside his finished meal and covered her hand. She looked so vulnerable sitting there, her large brown eyes as round as a child's. And she had an unconscious habit of tucking a bit of her hair behind her right ear that struck him as utterly appealing. She seemed to do it whenever she was nervous, and he wondered how he could set her at ease.

"What are you going to do this afternoon?" he asked as he stroked the velvety skin on the back of her hand. Was her palm as soft? His exploring fingers reported that it was.

"I'm going to buy a fish," she murmured absently.

"For dinner?"

"Smaller. I have to replace Mr. Beebles before my nephew finds out he died."

"I happen to know a pet store packed with tanks of Mr. Beebles."

"You'd go buy a goldfish with me?"

"Why not? You make it sound immoral. Of course, if it were an angelfish or a zebra it might be different. Certainly we ought to work our way up before we're seen out together buying guppies, but I think we can handle a goldfish."

Cassie laughed, and the lopsided dimple reappeared. Luke had the strangest urge to kiss it. "Ready to go?" he asked instead.

The pet shop was within walking distance, and he enjoyed having her beside him. Her skin was the deep creamy color only a brunette could have, and her hair was thick and glossy in the sunlight. He had always liked long hair, but most of the women he knew wore it short. Maureen's was scarcely longer than his own hair. He wondered if Cassie's was as soft as it looked.

They reached the pet store, and as Cassie studied the fish, Luke studied her. She fascinated him. The way her voice had a lilting tone when she spoke normally, and how it dipped huskily when she was nervous. The way she looked at him as if she couldn't quite decide if he was on the level. She was surprisingly shy, he decided. All the way to the restaurant she had scarcely spoken and had looked as if she would bolt and run if he spoke to her. After Maureen's polished sophistication, he found Cassie's naturalness very refreshing.

She wandered by a tank of goldfish and suddenly asked, "Do you plan to marry this Maureen? If you make up, I mean?"

Luke almost stumbled. He was accustomed to conversations that had beginnings, middles and ends. "No, I don't think I will."

"Why not?" She looked at him over the rim of the aquarium that separated them. "I mean, you sent her flowers and all. You must care for her."

"Sending flowers isn't as permanent a move as giving a ring, and I never gave her one of those. Why do you ask?"

"Because if you plan to marry Maureen, I shouldn't be here. I like you and I want to know where I stand. Okay?"

"I don't belong to anybody."

"Good. People don't belong *to* people, though," she corrected him. "Only *with* them. If Maureen is trying to own you, you're better off without her."

"She doesn't try to own me," Luke objected loyally. "We've had fun together, but there aren't any ties."

"Does she know that?" Again her chocolate eyes met his.

"I guess so. She says she doesn't ever want to see me again. That doesn't sound too permanent to me."

"Do you mind?"

Luke knew he should feel ill at ease over her probing questions, but somehow he wanted her to know about him. "No, I don't mind," he responded truthfully. He was suddenly aware that his relationship with Maureen had never been anything but tenuous. And now it was ended and he felt no loss.

Again Cassie smiled, revealing the deep dimple. "Good. I hate to meet people on the rebound." She ducked down to inspect the fish, and Luke bent over to look at her wavery form through the water.

"Do you always say whatever pops into your mind?" he asked.

"Not everything. Do you?"

"Of course not." There seemed to be no such thing as an ordinary conversation with her.

Cassie motioned to the clerk. "I'll take that little one swimming beside the castle."

The fish tried to elude capture, but Cassie insisted it was the only one that was the right size and color. Finally it was deposited in a plastic bag of water, and Cassie held out a bill to pay for it. Luke's grin returned as she turned to him and said, "Do you like cats? I hope you do, because I have one. His name is Phuzzbott and he came with the house."

"We're going to get along fine," Luke stated assuredly, meaning more than just the cat.

All the way back to the car and on the ride to Cassie's house, Luke listened to her animated conversation. Women in general had fascinated him since he discovered girls at the age of fourteen, but Cassie was in a class by herself. Everything she said was interesting and she seemed to be genuinely attentive to everything he told her. He could scarcely believe she hadn't been snapped up by now. The men in this town must be blind, he decided.

Her house was in an old section of two-story homes that were painted in an array of Easter-egg colors. The homes marched in a dignified line down the tree-shaded street to the water's edge. Beyond, the gray-green ocean rolled in an endless assault upon the minute beach and water-slicked black rocks. Cassie instructed him to pull into the last driveway on the block.

"You live here?" he asked as he stopped the car. "This is quite a house for a woman to take care of alone."

"It belonged to my great-aunt Cassandra," she explained as they got out. "She left it to me because I'm her namesake. I guess it would be smarter to sell it and get a smaller place or even an apartment, but I just can't do it. I've loved this old house all my life."

"If it were mine, I wouldn't consider selling it, either." He gazed out to the sea beyond the landscaped yard.

"The utility bills are a bear," she commented as they walked up the flagstone path. "But every time I watch a sunrise from my back window or hear the gulls, I know it's perfect for me." She smiled up at him. "When I was a girl my favorite stories were about the sea. It tells me secrets when I hear the waves roll." She grinned saucily. "Maybe it's because I'm a Pisces. What are you?"

"Scorpio."

Cassie's smile deepened, and she unlocked her front door. "Come in and make yourself at home while I fill the bowl for Beebles the Second."

Luke watched her go, admiring the unconscious sway of her hips. Talking to her was like playing verbal volleyball. He never knew what she would say next. He walked over to the sunny bay window and sat on the plump cushions to gaze at the sea. He, too, had a thing about water. The entire house and grounds had a pull for him, almost as if he had been there before.

Luke had grown up in a similar house, and he assumed this was the reason. An aura of stability pervaded the place, and he liked that. Dependability, solidness, security—these had always been important to him. This house seemed to embody them all.

Cassie came back into the room and put the fish, still in its plastic bag of water, into the half-filled bowl. "When the waters are the same temperature I'll pour him in. Terry will never know it's not the same fish."

"I like your house," Luke told her. "It seems so comfortable. I get the feeling I've been here before. Known you before."

"I have that same feeling about you," she replied softly. "Of course, that's impossible. If we had met before, I certainly would have remembered."

"Yes," he said thoughtfully. "We would have remembered. Will you have dinner with me?"

"I just had lunch with you."

"I know, but I plan to eat dinner as well, and I'd like for it to be with you." He found he couldn't look away from her beautiful brown eyes. Something deep within him was sparking to life, and it was only distantly related to physical desire. He wanted to stay with her and hear what she would say next.

Gradually, they both became aware of the phone ringing. Reluctantly, she pulled her eyes away and turned to answer it. As she did, she looked back at him as if to reassure herself he was really there.

He watched as her face went from an expectant

smile to a blank expression. "Could you repeat that more slowly?" he heard her say. A shocked look crossed her features and she paled, her knuckles ridging white as she gripped the receiver.

A small frown furrowed his forehead. Was it bad news? An accident, perhaps?

"Thank you," she murmured as she hung up. Slowly she shook her head and gestured unbelievingly. "They've been trying to reach me all day."

"What's wrong? Is someone hurt?"

"No," she answered numbly. "No, I just won the state lottery. They said they're holding a check for me. For seven million dollars."

2

Seven *million* dollars?" Luke asked dumfoundedly. "*Seven* million?"

Cassie nodded, looking at the phone as if she expected verification. "I wonder what I ought to do? I was going to have a tuna sandwich for dinner and watch a little TV tonight, but now . . ." She turned back to Luke. "I can't get the money until Monday, and I can't go out and celebrate on five dollars, and that's all I have in my purse." The immediate shock was fading, and she giggled. "What a ridiculous problem!"

He laughed with her. "Everyone should have such a quandary. Let me take you out to celebrate. You can't eat a sandwich alone on a night like this."

"You paid for lunch," she objected.

"You can take me out next time," he countered.

Giddiness was welling up in her. "Seven million . . . Luke! My ticket! She said I have to bring my ticket stub and identification with me when I go in to sign some forms." As she talked she rifled nervously through her purse, then extracted the green and gold Chance of a Lifetime ticket stub. As she clutched it tightly to her bosom, her bright smile faded to a frown. "Luke. What if it's not real! That could have been a prank call. Maybe someone is playing a trick on me!"

He crossed over to the phone and lifted it off the worn phone book. "Who called?"

"She said her name was Mrs. Westin. From the Massachusetts State Lottery Commission in Braintree."

Luke put the book down and called the information operator to get the number, then dialed. After a moment he said, "Mrs. Westin, please. Mrs. Westin? This is Luke Bennett. I'm calling to see if you just placed a call to Cassandra Collins in Plymouth." He paused to listen, then said, "Thank you. Good-bye." Hanging up, he lifted his eyes to Cassie. "No tuna fish for you tonight."

"No tuna?" she shrieked. "Good heavens! It's true? Not a joke?"

"It's true."

Cassie covered her mouth with her fingers and walked numbly to the window. Seven million dollars! She couldn't grasp the amount. "How big is seven million?" she asked as she stared sightlessly out to sea. "If I had it here, would it fit on the coffee table? Would it fill up the room? The house? How much is that?"

"I have no idea," Luke said with amusement.

"I ought to tell somebody. Mom. And Trina. And my friend Laura. Luke, I can't think. It's like my head is spinning in one direction and my brain in the other!"

"I'm having a little trouble taking it in myself," he admitted. "But the lady at the lottery office confirmed it."

"This is Saturday. What would anyone be doing working in a state office today? It must be a prank."

"No, it's surely on the level. I called and checked, remember?"

"That's right! It must be real!"

Cassie hurried back to the phone and punched out a series of numbers. "Busy!" Again she dialed. "No answer at Trina's. She may be over at Mom's. Damn! I win seven million dollars and I can't find anyone to tell about it!" Fingers flying, she called Laura's number. "Laura! Thank goodness you're home. I just won the state lottery! That's right. It's seven million dollars! Hello, Laura? Are you still there? No, I'm not kidding. Thanks. I've got to run now and tell Mom and Trina. Bye." Cassie carefully placed the ticket stub in her wallet, put her wallet in her purse and, with exaggerated motion, zipped it shut.

With a sigh, she smiled at Luke. "I feel better now. Come on." She grabbed her jacket from the hall tree. "I want you with me when I tell them. They'll never believe me. Besides, I'm too nervous to drive. You don't mind, do you? Oh, I hope not."

Cassie babbled nervously all the way to her mother's apartment. She had the oddest sensation of being unable to stop talking. She supposed she was in shock; she knew she was hyperventilating.

When they reached the apartment, Cassie took Luke's hand as naturally as if she had known him forever. "Now, don't be nervous," she told him. "Trina is here, because I saw her car, and sometimes Trina is very standoffish with strangers, but don't you let her worry you. That goes for Mom, too. Their bark is much worse than their bite." As she spoke she rang the bell, then opened the door and led him in. "Mom?"

"Back here," a voice called.

Cassie led Luke through a small living room crowded with furniture and dried floral arrangements and out to the kitchen. "Mom, Trina, this is Luke. I just won seven million dollars."

"My goodness, Cassie, how you do run on," the older woman said. She added, "I didn't catch his last name?"

A blank look crossed Cassie's face. Then, "Bennett! That's it, Bennett."

"You don't remember his name and yet you're hanging on to him for dear life?" Trina observed as she slid down from the padded leather barstool at the counter. To Luke she said, "I don't believe I've ever heard Cassie mention you."

"We only met today." He made no move to relinquish Cassie's hand. She seemed to need his support, and he could see why. Her family was formidable indeed. Both women looked coolly elegant and neither seemed to have paid any attention to

Cassie's announcement, or to Cassie herself. "Perhaps you didn't hear what Cassie said," he volunteered. "She just won the state lottery."

Now both pairs of eyes riveted to Cassie's nervously beaming face. She nodded eagerly. "Seven million dollars!"

"But you never buy a ticket," her mother protested.

"Trina talked me into it. Isn't this wonderful?"

"I'd say it's a great deal more than that," the older woman said.

"*Wonderful* is the biggest word I know right at the moment," Cassie answered.

"Are you certain there's no mistake?" Trina asked in a carefully bored voice. "Really, Cassie, you do tend to go off on tangents."

"There's no mistake," Cassie replied, clutching her purse. She was still smiling, but Luke saw some of the sparkle leave her eyes.

"I checked," he put in. "She won it all right. Seven million dollars."

"Seven . . . Are you somehow connected with this?" her mother asked suspiciously.

"No, no. He picked me up this afternoon and we had lunch," Cassie explained rather badly.

"Picked you up!" both women gasped together.

"She means I picked her up after she got off work," Luke added hastily. He could see why she hadn't wanted to come here alone.

"Assuming it's true," her mother said, "you won't get it all at once, you know. They dribble it out to you over twenty years or so."

"Not this one. This was a special lottery. I get it all in one lump."

"What will you do with all that money? You know you have no money sense," her mother chided her.

"I don't believe it," Trina stated flatly, and turned to pour herself some coffee.

"I guess I'll pay my phone bill," Cassie said in a joking tone as she forced a grin to her face to cover the exasperation she felt at her mother's criticism.

"That must be a whopper of a bill," Luke teased. He noticed her mother glance at him as if she wasn't amused, but he squeezed Cassie's hand reassuringly as she laughed.

"Don't giggle," her mother corrected automatically, "and quit doing that to your hair."

Cassie caught herself shoving her hair behind her ear and abruptly stopped. "Why aren't you excited?" she asked. "I thought you'd be jumping out of your skin over news like this." Disappointment colored her voice.

"I never 'jump out of my skin,'" her mother remarked dryly. "If it's true, you have my sincere congratulations," she said, but her body language contradicted her words.

"Well, I've got to go pick Terry up at school," Trina said. "I'll talk to you tomorrow, Mom. Mr. Bennett, it's been nice meeting you. Congratulations, Cassie." Her smile told them all that she wasn't believing it for a minute.

A small muscle tightened in Luke's jaw. How could they burst her balloon like that? "Are you ready,

Cassie? We have a lot of celebrating to do." He smiled down at her, trying to bring back the sparkle in her eyes.

She returned his smile uncertainly. All her life Trina had managed to squash Cassie's triumphs. Yet she could hardly believe it was happening with this. "I really did win it," she told her mother when Trina had gone.

"I believe you, dear," her mother soothed as if Cassie were a five-year-old reporting a flying saucer. "Coffee, Mr. Bennett?"

"No, thank you." Luke scarcely bothered to keep his tone civil. Was her family always so uncaring toward her? So deaf to her victories? Hell, this wasn't just a victory; she had won the whole ball of wax! A protective surge engulfed him and he put his arm around Cassie's waist. "Are you ready?" he asked.

Cassie nodded, not trusting herself to speak. It must all be a mistake, she told herself. Somehow she had misunderstood or something. She was just Cassie Collins who worked in the Daisy Dilly Flower Shoppe, not at all the sort of person to become a multimillionaire in the bat of an eye. She ran her fingers through her hair, looping it behind her ear.

Luke held out his hand to Mrs. Collins and shook the cool fingertips she offered him. "Nice meeting you," he said, not meaning a word of it.

"A pleasure, Mr. Bennett. Come again." She didn't sound as if she meant what she said, either.

As he walked Cassie back to his car, Luke hugged

her. "Hey, why the long face? You have reason to be happier than anyone in the whole state."

"It can't be real," she told him sadly. "Things like this don't happen to people like me."

"Didn't you say you had to go to Braintree to sign some papers?"

"Yes, but the lady said the banks won't be open until Monday morning, so I guess I should wait until then."

"Get in the car."

He drove the short distance to Braintree with grim determination, and after asking directions at two service stations, he pulled to a stop in front of a state building. "Get out and take your purse with you."

Cassie did as he said, but her steps flagged.

Luke took her hand and hurried her up to the front door. "I hope we're not too late."

"Luke, I'm too nervous. I'll just come back Monday."

"No, you won't. I can tell you won't believe it until you see written proof." The door opened beneath his hand and he hurried Cassie down the nearly deserted hallway.

Ten minutes later they returned, Cassie's face again wreathed in smiles. On the steps she paused and turned to him. "Thank you," she said simply.

He grinned down at her. "I've never kissed a millionaire before."

She put her arms around his neck and kissed him, oblivious to the fact that they were at a busy intersection, downtown, in broad daylight. In her purse she had a receipt for seven million dollars and instructions to give to her bank for the immediate transfer of the money to her account.

Cassie slept very little Saturday night even though Luke had brought her home fairly early following their celebration dinner. Sunday was just a blur. She took a cab to the flower shop to get her car, and then spent the remainder of the day gazing out to sea. Her brain seemed to have been short-circuited by the recent turn of events. It was as if all her dreams had come true, all at once. Luke was warm and sensitive and obviously he cared about her. It had been a long time since she'd met anyone who even came close to her ideal. And the sudden wealth! She couldn't comprehend what it meant to be a multimillionaire.

Monday morning at nine, Cassie was the first customer through the doors to Peabody Bank and Trust. Several hours later, Cassie left the bank and tugged open the protesting door of her car. Once inside, she sat for a minute, trying to digest all the banker had told her about investments and interest rates. Most of it had gone in one ear and out the other, but she resolved to go to the library in the near future and educate herself.

A cold front had gone through during the night, and even inside the car the air was chilly. Cassie jiggled the knobs on the heater and banged on the vent beneath the dash with the heel of her shoe. A blast of fetid air gushed into the car, chilling the interior even more, then belched to a stop. A grim smile played on Cassie's lips as she surveyed her ancient metal enemy. Now there was no reason to be at the car's mercy.

Talking to the engine in sugared tones, Cassie

coaxed life into the aged motor. There was a gleam of triumph in her eyes as she edged the protesting transmission from reverse to first gear. A smile played upon her lips as she lurched the car out onto the street.

Three blocks away she came to the spot she sought. Still talking encouragingly to the car, she turned into the parking lot of Bill Dill's Import Car Sales and coasted to a halt, letting the curb stop the car since the car's brakes were fading fast.

Row after row of shiny hoods and dazzling chrome grills glinted in the sun. As a farewell gesture, Cassie once more stuffed the gray tufts of cotton padding back into the torn seat upholstery, then kicked open the door. She refrained from telling the car what she thought of it, but she slammed the door with gusto.

A bored salesman stood just inside the double glass doors of the showroom. He had watched her arrival, and when she pushed open the door and entered, he pretended he was busy by polishing the distinctive hood ornament on one of the automobiles.

Cassie waited for a moment, hoping to catch his attention, but when he continued to ignore her, she looked around for another salesman. Three others stood near an office door, all discussing the weekend football game. With a shrug, Cassie started walking among the half dozen floor models.

After sliding in and out of all of them and carefully reading the list of features each offered, she walked back to the lone salesman and waited for him to notice her. When he began to polish the car door where her fingerprints had smudged the shiny handle, she reached out and touched his sleeve.

"Excuse me," she said. "Could you answer a question or two for me?"

"Certainly." He looked as if nothing would please him less than to talk to a woman who he plainly thought was only window-shopping.

Cassie had dealt with car salesmen and mechanics before, and she could spot the "little lady" routine from a mile away. She pointed toward a dark blue model. "What sort of gas mileage does the blue one get?"

"That's our top-of-the-line model," he told her in aloof tones. "It gets twenty-four on the road and twenty-one in town." He stopped as if she couldn't possibly expect him to volunteer more.

"Do you do your own service here, or would I have to take it somewhere else?"

He gave her a slightly offended glance. "We service our own automobiles."

She walked back to the car and looked it over again. The deep blue shine gave back a rounded reflection of herself and the showroom. Once more she slid inside and felt the soft glove leather of the comfortable seats and breathed in the scent of new-car elegance.

"What does this little knob do?"

"That's the cruise control."

Cassie rested her hands on the steering wheel and imagined herself driving it. "How do you get it out of the showroom?"

The salesman sighed. "Through that door back there. Are you and your husband interested in a new car? Perhaps he could come in after work and I'll show him what we have."

"No, *I'm* interested." She examined the array of dials and switches. It had every convenience she could imagine and some she had never considered. "If I bought this one, would I be able to take it out, say now, for instance?"

"That would be highly unlikely. Perhaps you didn't read the price on the window glass. This is our luxury model, the top of the line." He cast a deprecatory glare at her decrepit heap rusting away at the curb. "If that's the car you expect to use as a trade-in, I can't be very optimistic."

Cassie looked up in surprise. "You'd *give* me a trade-in?"

"That is our policy, but—"

"How much?"

He drew a long breath. "Fifty dollars."

A delighted smile lit her features. "That would be great. Frankly, I was expecting to have to hire someone to haul it away." She looked around proprietorially at the new car's luxurious interior. "I want this one."

"Most people do," he said dryly. "If you will have your husband . . ."

"I'm not married. How long will it take you to get it moved to the parking lot?"

His lips thinned in a harried gesture. "That's not the question. First we have to arrange for financing and check your credit, and—"

"That's not necessary," Cassie replied airily. "I'm going to pay cash for it."

The man studied her, sure now that he was being teased. "I see. Which bank will you be using?"

"I have the money right here." She got out of the car and smiled beatifically at the stunned salesman.

"You have this much money in your purse?" he gasped, tapping his fingernail against the price listed on the window.

Cassie leaned over and again read the figure. "Yes," she said as she straightened. "Let's go into your office. I want a written agreement about service warranties. And I believe it's customary to have a checkup done after it's been driven for a while. I might as well go ahead and make an appointment for that while I'm here."

After a long pause, the man called out in a squeaky voice, "Mr. Harris? Could you come here a minute?"

Once more Cassie had to explain that she wanted that particular car, not one in the back lot, and that she was prepared to pay cash if she could leave in it within an hour.

Fifty-five minutes later, Cassie drove away in her new car, not even bothering to look back at her previous transportation. The digital clock in the dashboard told her Luke must be getting home from work about then, so she smoothly maneuvered into the proper lane to head for his apartment.

Driving through the tree-lined streets, Cassie wondered if she was making a mistake. She hardly knew this Luke Bennett. True, she had spent most of Saturday with him, but before that she had never laid eyes on him, and he hadn't called her on Sunday. Cassie had an innate shyness when it came to relationships with men. Because of this she seldom dated, so she had little experience with which to assess her feelings for Luke.

Since Saturday, her thoughts had ricocheted wildly between having won the lottery and having met Luke. She recalled every word he had said to her and tried to read meaning into every possible nuance and inflection. And, in her imagination, she had spent the money in a multitude of ways from an African safari to wild shopping sprees in New York. Of the two, meeting Luke and winning the money, even Cassie couldn't have said which was the more exciting, because she could scarcely believe either had really happened to her. People like her didn't become multimillionaires overnight, nor did they meet men who looked like every woman's dream and had a personality to match. The banker had assured her the money was real. Now she had to see if Luke was.

His apartment complex, one of the newer and nicer ones in Plymouth, was ornamented with massive wrought-iron gates and improbable Southern-style columns. She pulled into one of the visitors' slots, carefully avoiding parking next to any other cars, then started roaming through courtyards in search of his apartment number among the profusion of identical doors.

She found number 419 beside a small swimming pool whose cerulean waters looked prohibitively cold in the autumn chill. Soon they would be winterizing the pool, she thought, as she shyly hesitated outside his door. She could turn and leave and he would never know the difference. If he called her again, great. If not, such was her usual luck. She watched a brilliantly hued fall leaf float down to the surface of the water as her desires wrestled with her shyness.

Stuffing her hands in the pockets of her blazer, she walked away three steps, then walked back. She wanted to see him. Never before had she taken the initiative in dealing with men, and her social life was dusty to prove it. Still, she didn't want a man she had to pursue. Again she walked purposefully away, only to stop abruptly within yards of his door. As if it were a magnet, it beckoned her, and she turned to frown at the brass knob. She wasn't a slave to her past, she informed herself. She could be assertive and not cause the sky to crash down. In every other aspect of her life she was very independent and self-assured. Only in dating relationships did she falter. She traced her steps back to the door.

Suddenly it opened and Luke stepped out, nearly knocking her down. "Cassie!" he exclaimed with surprise. "I've been trying to call you."

"You have?"

"The man at the flower shop said you weren't in today, and there was no answer at your house."

Relief flooded over her. He had tried to call. "I called in and took the day off. I had a lot of things to take care of."

She gazed up at him and felt the same expectant tingle she had experienced when she was with him before. He was clad in a nubby sweater of ivory cotton and jeans that hugged his muscled legs. The casual clothes made him even more handsome, and his voice was deeper than she remembered, its Southern accent more sensual.

"Would you like to go to the park?" she asked breathlessly. "It won't be dark for a little while yet, and it is a beautiful afternoon," she added as if he might need inducement. "Unless, of course, you had other plans. I mean, you were on your way out. I'll bet I came at a bad time. You have other plans. It's my fault for dropping by and I won't do it again. I never do, really. Maybe some other time." She was backing away as she talked, her timidness engulfing her.

"Hold it. You just had an entire conversation all by yourself." He grinned at her as he said, "I'd like to go to the park. As for my other plans, I was only going to the front building to get my mail. Just let me get my jacket."

Cassie exhaled the breath she hadn't realized she was holding. She hadn't done so badly after all.

Luke returned immediately, wearing a tan leather coat. "I'm ready if you are."

"You look nice," Cassie said, then blushed. Her old habit of saying whatever crossed her mind had embarrassed her again.

"Thanks. I was about to say the same thing about you." He took her arm to direct her to his car.

"Oh, could we go in my car? I just bought it. That's one of the reasons I came by unexpectedly. I wanted to show it to you. I guess that was pretty presumptuous of me, wasn't it? After all, we hardly know each other. Maybe I should just . . ."

"Do you do that often?" he asked with interest.

"What?"

"Scold yourself and then chase yourself off. Personally, I'm glad you're here."

"You are?"

"That's why I was trying to call you. To ask you out."

"You were?"

"I'm glad you came by. I like a woman who'll take the initiative."

"You do?" She stared up at him, wondering if many men felt that way.

"Sure. It's just as important to me to know you're interested as it is for you to know I am."

"I never thought of it like that." They walked to the sleek blue car and she gestured proudly. "There it is."

Luke gave a low whistle. "You have fantastic taste in cars. That's a real beauty."

"Wait until you see all the gadgets inside. I haven't figured out half of them."

They rode to the park in luxurious comfort, Cassie enjoying the thrill of knowing her car would be able to leave each stop sign without stalling, and Luke engrossed in helping her figure out all the knobs and dials on the dashboard. Luke's Audi was a very nice car, but this one was elegant.

"This car does everything but talk," he exclaimed admiringly.

"There may be a button for that, too."

She turned down a quiet side street and parked near a jumble of swings and picnic tables. They got out, and when Luke held out his hand to her, she placed hers in it with no shyness at all. Their feet made rustling sounds in the colorful carpet of leaves, and all around could be heard the happy shrieks of children at play.

"I haven't been here in a long time," Luke said as they strolled down to the pond. "I'm glad you suggested it. Seems like I've been caught up in work these last few months and haven't taken time to even look at roses, much less smell them."

"You should work where I do," Cassie teased. "I come here often. I've always liked parks—being outside, breathing fresh air. I even come in the wintertime." She took a deep breath. "Autumn smells so nice and clean. I think it may be my favorite season."

"Mine, too."

"Spring is my other favorite." She smiled up at him. "I'm flexible."

The pond's calm water reflected the rosy glow of the evening sky and rippled lazily against the grassy shore. Cassie tossed in a pebble and watched the concentric circles roll out and fade away in the peaceful water.

"I'd like to be like that," she commented. "Smooth and unruffled like the water of this pond. Nothing really bothers it. You could toss a boulder in it and it would smooth back out again."

Luke looked at her curiously. One minute she seemed as shy and uncertain of herself as a young girl; the next she was revealing a facet from deep within. "You remind me more of a mountain stream," he said. "All bubbly and as apt to go one way as the other."

She nodded and sighed. "Trina is like a lake. Always tranquil and never going off on tangents."

"Sometimes tranquillity can be dull." Luke hadn't

been all that impressed with Cassie's sister—or with her mother, for that matter.

"You, on the other hand, are like a river," Cassie offered. "Deep and steady and with a strong current." She looked up at him from the corner of her eye and added, "I've always liked rivers."

Luke smiled at her oblique compliment. He could never anticipate what she would say next. "Do you think having all this money is going to change you?"

"Why?"

"Because if it does, it would be a real shame." The expression in his eyes gave the words a very intimate tone, as did his soft voice.

Cassie looked back at the water. "It won't change me." She tossed in another pebble and frowned slightly. "The newspaper interviewed me this morning before I went to the bank. Tomorrow I'm to be on the five o'clock talk show on television. I have to admit I'm a little nervous about that. What if I say something dumb or get an eyelash in my eye or something?"

"You'll be fine. I'll get home in time to watch."

"Oh, don't do that. If I know you're watching, I'll *really* get nervous. No, I know. Watch, but don't tell me. No, then I'd know you did since I just told you to. Don't watch. I would like for you to see it, though."

Luke burst out laughing. "You must not ever get lonely. You always have yourself to talk to."

Cassie smiled wryly. "You'd be surprised, Luke. You really would."

"By the way, if you need the name of an accountant

to help you figure out what to do with all that money, I'll be happy to help you find one. Or do you already have someone to advise you?"

More advice she didn't need. She'd had people trying to tell her what to do all her life. Instead of answering, she cried out, "Look! There's the balloon man. Come on!"

She pulled him into a jog and they hurried over to the bored-looking vendor. "How much for your balloons?"

"The plain ones are a dollar; the shiny ones are three," he answered.

"I mean, how much for all of them?" Cassie asked as she fished in her purse for her billfold.

"All?" The man looked from her to the mass of balloons and back again. "A hundred bucks, maybe?" Obviously he had never been asked that question before.

"I'll take them." Cassie gave him a hundred-dollar bill and took the wad of strings from him. "Thanks, and have a good evening," she called over her shoulder as she nudged Luke toward the playground.

Enjoying herself immensely, Cassie went from child to child, bestowing balloons on everyone. Luke followed, watching her with wonder. He couldn't imagine anyone else doing something like this.

When all the balloons were gone, Cassie turned her radiant face to him. "There! I've always wanted to do that."

"Lady, I've got to hand it to you," he said with a

grin. "You've got flair." He took her hand again. As they wandered back to her car, he hoped she had discernment as well. Otherwise she would go through her fortune like a whistle through the wind. A flood of protectiveness washed over him, warming him, and he squeezed her hand.

3

Cassie," Elwin Glass hissed. "There's someone to see you. Again."

Cassie let her hands rest on the worn work counter and sighed. She was still only half-finished with the Smythtons' get-well bouquet and it was almost quitting time. "Are you sure they want me? I have to get this finished and I can't work late tonight."

"Believe me, they want you." Her boss wrinkled his receding hairline and pursed his thin lips. A sure sign of anger, as Cassie well knew.

"All right." For the tenth time that day, Cassie returned her work to the glass refrigerated case and wiped the flecks of fern and styrofoam from her fingers. "Mr. Glass, I didn't expect—"

"Just get out front and see what this one wants." His words were clipped and unfriendly.

Cassie shouldered through the red lacquered batwing doors that screened the workroom from the showroom, and walked over to the woman hovering by the cash register. She had lank hair and an imploring stance; both her bony hands gripped a handwoven purse. Cassie felt a sinking sensation; she had dealt with others just like this one every day since she won the lottery the week before, and it had been difficult every time. "Yes?" she asked warily. "I'm Cassie Collins."

"It's so good to meet you," the woman said in low, earnest tones. "We've never met. My name is Freedom Bonner."

Freedom? Cassie thought.

"I heard about your good fortune from the newspaper a few days ago, and I want to plead our cause with you."

"What cause is that?" Cassie met the woman's large spaniel eyes.

"I'm the representative for the Boston chapter of Save the Whales. It's a terribly worthy organization."

Cassie exhaled with relief. "I've contributed to that cause for quite a while now, and I completely agree with you." She smiled disarmingly. Over the past week she had been urged to contribute to some organizations she was positive had to be fakes and a few that were unpatriotic at the very least. This one at least was valid and worthwhile.

Despite Cassie's statement, the woman continued pleading in desperate tones as if Cassie, and Cassie alone, could save the endangered whales. "Just think what seven million dollars could do for our cause!

Why, with that kind of money we could save them all!"

Behind her Cassie heard the grating of clay flower pots being shoved around. Turning to the woman, she said, "I appreciate your viewpoint, but I really can't talk about it. I have to get back to work now." She steered the woman toward the door as a man entered. "I promise you I'll continue to send donations to your cause."

"But seven million—"

"I know. I'll keep that in mind." She firmly piloted the woman out and closed the door. To the new customer, she turned a welcoming smile. "May I help you?"

"You're the woman that won the lottery? Yeah! I saw you on TV! You're not as tall as I expected. Say, me and my brother want to make you our partner in a used-car franchise—"

"No," Cassie said bluntly.

"You don't understand. This is on the level. A deal like this could double your money in a year's time, maybe two."

"No."

"We would be the main bosses. We'd handle the business since we know that part so well. All you have to do is back us. What do you say?"

"No!"

"Think it over," he suggested as she opened the door and waited for him to leave. "Don't answer now if you don't want to. We'll check back."

Cassie closed the door unnecessarily hard behind

him. From the workroom came the grating of more pots being moved. She looked toward the red doors with trepidation. When Elwin became so upset that he shifted pots, he was upset indeed.

Glancing at the daisy-shaped clock on the wall, Cassie hurried to the back. Luke was taking her to a party that night, and she had no time to work late. "I'm sorry about that," she apologized as she took the flowers out of the cooler again. The almost visible fragrance of cold flower scents followed her to the workbench.

"That's been going on for a week now," Elwin complained. "When will these interruptions stop?"

"Mr. Glass, I wish I knew! They bother me at least as much as they do you."

"Doubtful." Elwin spun a pot of begonias toward the window, using such force that the leaves twitched and pink petals rained onto the counter top.

"When I bought that ticket to the lottery I hardly expected to win. I had never bought one before in my life! I certainly had no idea that everyone on the East Coast would come asking me to give my money to them!"

Elwin, who had spent hundreds of dollars on lottery tickets over the years, snorted in disbelief. "I've always heard those drawings are rigged."

Cassie stared at him, then jabbed a carnation into the nest of ferns and roses. She had heard that accusation before, too. "At least you don't have to worry about me asking you for a raise," she tried to joke."

Instead of smiling, Elwin frowned. "I've been meaning to talk to you about that. I'd like for you to take a cut in salary."

"A cut in salary! Why!"

"You already make more than my other two helpers."

"They only work after school three days a week! I'm your full-time manager!"

"It's not like you need the money," Elwin snorted as he fixed her with a cold glare.

"That's not the point! It's the principle. You can't cut my pay just because I don't need it!"

"I've been considering letting you go altogether," he baited with studied casualness as he fluffed the begonia leaves.

"*Fire* me? On what grounds?"

"It's a moral issue. By letting you go, I can hire someone who needs the money. Unlike you."

"But I love this job! And I'm good at it—you know I am!"

Elwin's thin lips lifted in a mean little smile as if he had at last drawn blood. "Someone else might be better."

Cassie glared at him. "That's discrimination! You know it is."

"But no one *cares* if the rich are discriminated against," he informed her in syrupy syllables.

Uncertainly, Cassie turned back to the arrangement. She had never thought about it in those terms before. The very rich were a minority no one wanted to protect.

The faded plastic clock above the door told her it

was five o'clock. Hastily Cassie pushed some more carnations in the arrangement and added a pink bow on which was stapled the card. It wasn't her best effort, but it was all she could do at that point. "Finished," she announced.

"Too many carnations," Elwin judged, flicking one out and viewing the arrangement as if it were rather distasteful. "I suppose it will have to do. Deliver it on your way home, won't you?"

Seething, Cassie returned the unused carnations to the cooler. "All right, but you know that isn't part of my job."

"For however long *that* may last." Having found her tender spot, Elwin wasn't in any hurry to stop probing it.

Cassie took off the shiny red apron and thrust it over the peg on the wall. After shrugging into her coat, she grabbed up the flowers and her purse and left without so much as a good-bye. She had already said more to her boss than she had intended, and it was not until she had left the shop that she realized she would no longer have to put up with his overbearing tactics. She had no intention of quitting her job; she loved working with flowers and enjoyed the contact with people it afforded her. But the money did give her a certain sense of freedom that she had never felt before.

After delivering the flowers to the hospital, Cassie headed for home. Traffic was heavy, as it usually was on a Friday night, and she needed all her attention to maneuver through the congestion, but she no longer needed to plan where she could safely leave her car if it quit. Those days were over.

When she reached home she hurried inside. A cold front was blowing through town, and the wind already carried the threat of rain. The ocean, her favorite barometer, was flat and slate gray. By dawn she would need a fire.

She gave Mr. Beebles a cursory glance to see he was still afloat, so to speak, then poured a measure of dry food for her cat.

"I've got a heavy date tonight, Phuzzbott," she said as she stroked his long fur. "You stay inside where it's warm." He arched his back and purred before wholeheartedly attacking the bowl of food. Phuzzbott was a cat who loved comfort and rarely went out except on the most perfect of days, a pioneer spirit being missing from his nature.

Cassie bathed quickly and washed her hair even though she was pressed for time. She had never met Luke's friends and she wanted to make a good impression. True, this was an office party and not a strictly social gathering, but all the more reason to make him proud of her.

She blew her hair dry as she craned her neck around her closet door. At last she located her emerald green dress in the very back. Kneeling and peering through her tumbling, air-ruffled hair, she groped for her heels.

Somehow she managed to put on makeup, twist her hair into a high Grecian knot on the crown of her head, and dress before the doorbell rang. She glanced critically at the mirror on her closet door before slamming the door shut. The dress was demure and simple from the front. It's soft wool clung to her full breasts and accentuated her slender waist before belling out into a graceful skirt. The neckline made a backdrop for her simple pearl drop that matched her earrings, and the sleeves molded her arms. The back of the dress plunged in a deep vee to her waist.

Cassie opened the door to Luke and he entered on an autumn-scented wind. "Looks like a storm may be building," he said; then his eyes widened and his slow grin spread across his face. "You look great!"

"Thank you." Cassie smiled, turning to get her evening wrap. "I'm ready if you are."

"Wait. Turn around again."

She faced away from him, wondering if she had left a tag exposed or a button undone. When he failed to speak, she asked, "Are you still back there? What's wrong?"

"Absolutely nothing. I was just enjoying the view." He put his fingers caressingly on the wispy curls at the nape of her neck and let them stroke down the faint indentation of her spine to her waist.

A delicious shiver tingled through her, and she smiled over her shoulder at him. "Am I overdressed? Underdressed?"

"I wouldn't change a stitch." His admiring eyes confirmed his words. "At least not at the moment."

Cassie's eyes dropped, and she tried to conquer her shyness. She had known this was a dress to bewitch and seduce. She just hadn't expected such immediate success. "We had better be going or we'll be late."

"I don't mind." His fingers were working their way

back up, reveling in her warm skin. Then he noticed how quiet she'd become and he stopped. "Hey," he said softly, turning her to face him. "Did I upset you?"

A detestable blush colored her cheeks. "No, I'm not upset. I just don't want you to think, well, you know, that I'm promising there will be a 'later.'"

"That's not what I thought or what I meant," he assured her. "It's no secret how I feel, but I'm not presuming anything."

Relief warmed Cassie and she relaxed into a smile. She had only been seriously involved once before, and the man had taken her choice of clothing as a direct announcement of her intention. Cassie was much too mercurial to know at the beginning of an evening how she would feel at its end. This had led to many arguments and the accusation that she was a tease, when nothing was further from the truth. "I like you," she said unexpectedly.

"I like you, too." He paused as if he wanted to say more, then grinned. "Your cloak, madam. The carriage awaits."

Cassie furled her white wool wrap over her shoulders and they stepped out into the rapidly cooling darkness. "I may wish I had worn my long johns before we get back. That wind is cold!"

Luke laughed at the image of Cassie swathed in thermal underwear from ankle to neck beneath her sexy dress. "Do you want to get a heavier coat?"

"No, I'm cold but fashionable."

"I'll do my best to keep you warm," he promised as he opened the car door for her.

Cassie hadn't the slightest doubt he could do that.

His touch on her bare skin had warmed her to the boiling point already. Her emotions were on a seesaw. She wanted him, wanted to love him, yet her innate shyness masked her desire. At times she felt as if there were another Cassie waiting just below her surface for a kiss, a touch, to bring her to life. The fantasy softened Cassie's features in a smile. She had loved that other man, but he had not stirred such wildly wanton feelings in her. Once again her active imagination was working full speed.

The party was under way when they arrived, and Cassie heard a jovial babble of voices roll out to meet them when the hostess opened the door. Cassie smiled and nodded her way through a flurry of introductions. She had never been terrific at remembering names, and soon they were all a blur to her.

"So you're Cassie," a middle-aged man observed over the rim of his glass of bourbon. "Luke has talked a lot about you. It's easy to see why."

"Oh?" Cassie never knew how to answer a comment such as that.

"Yeah, winning all that money must have really been something," the man continued. "I wish I knew a good-looking chick with millions of dollars." He made a show of flinching when his wife punched him in the arm.

"That's what I really call job security," the man beside him joked. "If Luke gets laid off, she can support him better than he's used to supporting himself." The two men roared together.

Luke's hand tightened on her elbow and he led her away without hesitation. His eyes had a flinty shine, and Cassie glanced over her shoulder at the two men, who were still laughing loudly. "Ignore them. They're the office clowns. I should have expected them to say something offensive."

"That's all right. I've heard comments similar to those all week." With a sharp twinge of disappointment, she gave up hoping tonight would be different.

Luke wove his way through the crowd to the bar and got them each a gin and tonic. Cassie sipped her drink, wishing she found it easier to meet people.

"Luke! Glad you could make it. This must be Cassie?"

She turned, anticipating another slap about her money, but this time Luke was relaxed and smiling.

"Cassie, I want you to meet my friend, Skip Masterson, and his wife, Kelley. Skip and I started out at Pan-Ways at the same time."

The couple looked friendly, and Cassie found herself relaxing for the first time since she had walked in. Kelley held her husband's hand, causing Cassie to guess they were newlyweds. Neither mentioned her money.

"I'm glad to meet you," Skip told her. "Luke has talked about you all week. From the glowing account, I was beginning to think you were a figment of his imagination. Now I see he was making understatements." He wiggled his eyebrows at Cassie in a parody of a flirtation.

"Back off, buddy, or I'll have Kelley punch you out," Luke growled in pretended anger. Cassie could tell he and Skip were accustomed to teasing banter.

"Really, you two!" Kelley scolded playfully. To Cassie she said, "It's always something with them. Just ignore them and they'll usually behave."

"But not always," Skip added, leaning over and gnawing at his wife's neck. Kelley squealed and swatted him with her purse.

"Newlyweds," Luke confirmed to Cassie. "They're pretty embarrassing, but I tolerate them."

Cassie laughed at his sanctimonious expression as much as at his uninhibited friends. Somehow she had expected Luke's friends to be more conservative and proper, all the things she tried so hard to be and had always failed so noticeably to achieve.

"Skip, stay!" Kelley commanded as if he were a misbehaving puppy. "Cassie, he isn't always like this." A twinkle showed in her eyes. "Sometimes he's worse. If you think you can stand it, however, we would like for you and Luke to have dinner with us."

Before they could set a date, a large man joined them. At once Cassie felt a tightness in the small group. Although the men still smiled, their expressions had hardened.

"Cassie, I'd like to introduce our boss, Mr. Merriweather," Luke said politely but with a lack of enthusiasm. "This is Cassie Collins."

"Hello," she responded, offering him her hand.

He took only her fingers, pressed them, and released them. "So you're the little lady I've been reading about in the paper," he said, a thoughtful note in his voice. "I saw you on television. Somehow I expected you to be taller."

"I am," she said with a smile. "It's the lighting in here that makes me look short." She heard Kelley catch a giggle before it could escape.

Mr. Merriweather blinked as the joke sailed cleanly over his balding head. "I suppose you've decided how to invest it," he said quite seriously. "Money like that should be used, not left lying fallow." To Luke, he said, "Would you get me a scotch on the rocks? I'll keep Miss Collins company."

Luke looked as if he might refuse, but finally nodded. "I'll be right back, Cassie."

As soon as Luke left, his boss steered Cassie away from Kelley and Skip and said, "It's not widely known, but I happen to have a business on the side." He favored her with a wintery smile. "I'm in commercial real estate. It's as solid a shelter as there can be."

"Oh?" Cassie sucked in a deep breath because she knew what was coming.

"Last week I heard about a deal I know you'll be interested in. I have a chance to buy some estate property near downtown. Because it's through a friend, he won't sell to anyone but me, but his price is steep. Now, if you would back me, I could buy the land, tear down the old house on it and put up a high-rise apartment and maybe a few small stores as well. You'd get your investment back in no time and make a tidy profit."

"Aren't there enough apartments around here already?" she hedged.

"There's never enough. You've got to get out there and make that money work!" he said with the enthusiasm of a football coach giving a pregame pep talk.

At that point Luke found them and handed his boss the glass. "Here's your scotch."

"I'm really not interested, Mr. Merriweather," Cassie said. "I haven't decided what to do with the money, but that sounds too foreign to me."

"Foreign? It's good solid business. Let me explain it to you again."

"No, thank you." She wished Mr. Merriweather weren't Luke's boss so she could be more adamant. "It's a nice party," she said in hopes of changing the subject. Even if she would have wanted to invest in his project, his derogatory comment had convinced her to avoid him.

"I don't think you understand my concept," Mr. Merriweather persisted. "I plan big things here."

"She said no," Luke put in quietly.

"This doesn't concern you, Bennett. Not unless you plan to marry the little lady." A falsely jovial smile rounded his jowls.

Cassie had had enough; she wasn't going to be talked down to. "Call me 'little lady' one more time and I'll stuff the money up your nose," she offered sweetly. Suddenly remembering that she was talking to Luke's boss, she tightly clamped her mouth and turned to check Luke's expression. Had she committed a faux pas? The man was not Elwin Glass.

Luke was gazing down at her with admiration. To Merriweather he said, "We were talking with Skip and his wife when you came up. I see them over by the punch bowl. If you will excuse us . . ." Luke casually offered Cassie his arm and led her away.

Mr. Merriweather could have let them go unobtrusively, but he had come early to the party and was already well acquainted with the bottle of scotch. "Hold on! You can't walk away from me. Now, Miss Collins, you're throwing away a big opportunity. I can make you a multimillionaire!"

"I already am one," Cassie reminded him.

"She said no," Luke repeated in a firmer voice. "Let's just drop it."

"Sure, you say that! You've got your nest feathered, don't you!" Merriweather was plainly under the influence of his previous drinks.

Luke's body tensed and Cassie caught his clenched hand. Before he could react to Merriweather's insinuations, she said, "Let's go." When Luke continued to glare at the older man, she grabbed his arm and pulled him away. "Let's go *now!*"

Somehow they got across the room as word of the argument spread about them. Cassie's cheeks flamed with anger, but she kept her head proudly erect. She groped through the pile of wraps in the front bedroom until she found her shawl, then hurried to rejoin Luke, who was saying good-bye to their host and hostess.

Before they could escape, Merriweather shouldered through the crowd. Pointing at Luke, he made no effort to lower his voice. "You better talk to her, Bennett. You better change her mind!"

Luke's face hardened and he took a step toward the man. "Listen here, you—"

"Luke!" Cassie whirled to face him. "Let's leave!"

Reluctantly, he let her pull him out into the cold night. Behind her she could hear the shocked and gossiping voices. When he paused, she caught his arm more firmly. "Come on. It's not worth losing your job over."

"I'm not so sure about that."

"Nonsense," she managed to tease. "We can't have astronauts flying around naked in space just because I don't want to invest in a high-rise."

"I don't want anyone talking to you like that," Luke growled protectively. "If I didn't think he was too drunk to know what he was doing, I'd quit anyway."

"Luke, I don't want you quitting your job because of me. Besides, how many places can you find a job designing space suits? It's not that big a deal."

Luke didn't agree, but she kept moving him toward the car. Now that it was all over, Cassie felt shaken. The money certainly brought out qualities she had never before seen in people. She had never dreamed being rich could cause so many problems.

They drove back to her house, neither speaking. Cassie glanced at Luke as the streetlights lit his face then receded into the darkness. Was he sorry he had taken her to the party? This must have been even more embarrassing to him; he had to work with these people every day.

He turned in her drive and switched off the motor. After a pause, he said, "Cassie, I'm sorry. I don't know how to fix it and yet I want to. If I had known how this was going to turn out, I'd never have considered going to that party."

"I know that."

He faced her in the shadowy interior of the car. "It's

still early. Do you want to go dancing, or to a late movie?"

"No." She couldn't bear to be around more people after the unpleasant scene. "Do you know what I really want to do?"

"Tell me."

"I want us to go inside, make popcorn, and watch TV in front of a roaring fire."

He pretended he had to consider this seriously before he could answer. "*Buttered* popcorn?"

She nodded. "With salt. Eaten from a big plastic mixing bowl."

"The bowl convinced me. Let's go."

They walked briskly through the windy cold and hurried into the warmth of the house. Phuzzbott raised his broad head sleepily and blinked a welcome to them before settling back down in his favorite sleep position.

Luke looked from the contented cat to the lazily drifting fish. "What keeps the cat from snacking on Mr. Beebles?"

"As long as the fish stays in the bowl, he's safe. Phuzzbott isn't into water sports." Cassie grinned, giving the cat—who ignored her—an affectionate pat. "How are you at making fires?"

"I wasn't a boy scout for nothing. Where would you like one?" He surveyed the room as if anywhere might be suitable to him.

"In the hearth, please. I'm very traditional. I'll make the popcorn."

By the time she returned, a steady blaze was

crackling and a coziness pervaded the room. She paused at the door, taking in the sight of Luke in shirt sleeves, his suit coat casually hung on the hall tree, as he searched for a movie on the television set. Phuzzbott had left the chair and was sprawled across the hearth, soaking up warmth and comfort. The antique mantel clock struck the half hour, its mellow notes blending with the harmonious scene. Cassie found herself memorizing the scene as one she would treasure. Luke fit here so well, she realized she wanted him here on a permanent basis. Up until now she hadn't let herself admit how much he meant to her. Nervously she said, "Popcorn?"

Luke looked up and nodded. "It smells great. Do you like old movies?"

"Yes, I do." She tried to see through his casual words. Did he care for her? Surely someone as wonderful as Luke must be destined for a perfect woman, not someone like herself.

"Good. *The African Queen* just started." He motioned for her to join him on the couch. "Are you planning to hoard all the popcorn for yourself?"

She sat beside him and kicked off her shoes. Never had she known anyone who put her more at ease.

"The Germans just killed the missionary brother, and Katharine Hepburn is trying to get Bogey to take her down the river," he neatly synopsized the story for her.

Cassie curled against his side as he put his arm around her to pull her close, the popcorn cradled on their laps between them. He surprised her by feeding her a bite instead of himself, though his eyes never left the screen. She returned the favor, putting the choicest bit of corn to his lips.

For a moment their eyes met and lingered; then Luke winked sexily at her and she understood. Earlier she had been afraid her seductive dress would promise more than she might be willing to give, but his expression eased that apprehension. He seemed to be showing her that any commitment they might make to each other would be one of the head as well as the heart.

"I'm looking for love, not lust," he said as if the previous exchange had been verbal.

Cassie smiled and snuggled closer. Whatever else he might become, Luke was her friend.

Together they cheered on the intrepid adventurers on the screen and munched popcorn as their stockinged feet soaked up warmth from the fire. By the time Bogey and Hepburn sank the German ship, Cassie knew she was in love.

"I guess I ought to go," Luke said as the credits rolled over the screen.

"It's not late."

He gazed deeply into her eyes. "Maybe one more movie."

She beamed. "I'll make more popcorn."

By the end of the next film, they had eaten the popcorn, emptied her cookie jar, and polished off two soft drinks apiece. And Cassie was pretty sure Luke was in love as well.

They strolled arm in arm to the front door, Cassie's

bare feet making her even shorter. He put on his coat with slow movements, postponing leaving for as long as possible. "Well," he said as the national anthem sounded over the television. "I guess that's all the movies."

She nodded reluctantly. "I think I'll sign up for cable tomorrow. Then we can eat popcorn around the clock."

He chuckled and pulled her close. "I'm glad I know you, Cassie."

"I am, too. That I know you, that is."

Slowly he lowered his head, and his lips, still slightly salty from the popcorn, brushed hers experimentally. Then he pulled her against him, curving her willing body up to meet his. His mouth was velvet on hers, and she found the room seemed to dip and spin about her as he loved her with a kiss such as she had never experienced before.

Cassie threaded her fingers through his thick hair and opened her lips to his seeking tongue. She heard a soft moan as warmth spread through her body, and was surprised to discover the sound was her own.

At length he released her and looked down at her with eyes grown so dark as to be nearly black. Cassie knew the surrendering triumph of love being returned, though no words were spoken.

At last he said, "Can I see you tomorrow?"

Slowly she nodded, afraid to move too fast for fear of changing the glimmering wonder of the moment. "If you'll come over about five, we can walk on the beach. I'll cook supper."

"Perfect."

Again he kissed her, and when he released her and left, Cassie leaned limply against the door, a grin tilting her dewy lips. Even if the words hadn't been spoken, her heart had listened and responded to his.

4

Cassie watched Elwin work ruthlessly, pinching back the begonias while his lower lip protruded in anger. Even the bald spot on top of his head seemed to shine with bad temper. The worst part was that she couldn't blame him.

The entire morning had been a repeat of the day before. Everyone in Plymouth and the surrounding towns seemed to have a get-rich-quick scheme that included her money. A large number of them had come to the flower shop to tell her in detail of their ideas, even though Cassie made it clear she wasn't interested. Elwin had been simmering ever since.

"Mr. Glass?" she ventured. "Do you want me to rotate the ferns?" She knew the answer but hoped to placate him by asking his advice.

"Leave them where they are."

"Pardon?" She was quite sure the delicate plants were too near the north windows, which tended to have a draft. "It's cold today and you know how temperamental a fern is."

"I said leave them alone!" he spewed in a spiteful whine. "Honestly! I have to tell you everything!"

Cassie frowned. Usually, he complained over her independence and accused her of trying to take over the shop. With a shrug, she went back to her task of tying bows to the sharp green sticks she used in the arrangements. They weren't her ferns, after all. Elwin usually left early on a Saturday and she could move the ferns after he was gone.

The little brass bell over the shop door jangled and Cassie leaned forward to look into the showroom. Elwin greeted the man, who was dressed in worn jeans, a black turtleneck sweater and a threadbare denim vest. He didn't look like a typical customer for the flower shop, and Cassie moved uneasily.

"Cassie!" Elwin barked. "Someone to see you!"

With trepidation, Cassie put down her scissors and straightened the red slickered apron as she went to see what it was. "Yes?"

"You're Cassie Collins?" The young man had a hungry look about him and the flat eyes of a fanatic.

She nodded as a couple she knew entered the shop. Bona fide customers, she thought. Maybe they would draw Elwin's attention until she could get rid of this fruitcake.

"You don't know me. I'm Samuel. You've got to help me." His voice was constrained and mumbling.

Get rid of him, she warned herself. "I'm afraid you've come to the wrong place, Mr. Samuel," she said firmly.

"Not Mister, just Samuel. We have only one name." He gave her a flicker of a smile that somehow made him seem even more intense. "It's upon us, you know. The end of the world."

Cassie stared blankly at him. This was a new angle, at least.

"We've been given a revelation." Before she could stop him, he took her hand and examined her thumb. Pointing to a pale scar, he said, "Take heart. You're one of the chosen. We're identified by the scar on our right thumbs. See? Here's mine."

"Out!" Cassie said, pointing at the door. She knew Elwin hadn't missed a syllable of the exchange. "Get out and take your scar with you."

"They said you would be startled at first," he persisted with the odd, flickering smile. "But I'm to tell you that we are to escape the earth's destruction by colonizing the planet Vulcan—earth's twin, opposite the sun. A spaceship costs seven million dollars."

"Out!" Cassie took his ragged lapel between her thumb (the scarred one) and forefinger and pulled him toward the door. "Tell *them* I'm not going and not to send you back."

Huffily Samuel exited, retorting, "Nothing can save the earth now!"

Ignoring his staring customers, Elwin stalked over to her. "That does it. You're fired!"

"But it wasn't my fault!" Cassie argued.

"If you weren't here, that kook would never have

come in here. I run a decent, respectable business!" This last was for the benefit of the ogling customers. "I won't have you drawing in every weirdo on the East Coast!"

"I got rid of him!"

"You've disrupted my business. Take off that apron and get out of my store!" Elwin bellowed.

Cassie stared at him. A knotted vein throbbed in his temple, and his eyes were glassy. He seemed to be serious. "I really am fired?" she asked to be sure.

"If you aren't gone in five minutes I'll . . . I'll do something drastic!"

"But you don't have anyone to take my place, and I know more than both your part-time workers put together. You can't just fire me like this!"

"Yes, I can. I'm doing the world a public service. You don't need a job and there are hundreds that do. Maybe thousands! By firing you I can hire someone who needs work."

"But I'm *good* at my work! And I like my job! I don't just goof off and collect my paycheck!"

"Get out of here!" The vein turned rosy and threatened to burst.

Cassie decided that when logic failed, retreat wasn't out of order. With a jerk, she removed the red apron and tossed it onto the cash register. "Daisy Dilly is a dumb name," she called back as a parting shot, then hurried out the back door before he could explode.

This was so totally wrong and unexpected that Cassie didn't know whether to be angry or hurt. How could Elwin Glass be so heartless? None of what happened had been her fault. She hadn't asked those people to come to the store to disrupt business. When she thought about how he had fired her in front of those customers, a wave of embarrassment and humiliation washed over her. She'd never been fired before. Not ever.

Settling on anger as the least threatening emotion for the moment, she started her car and aimlessly drove away from the flower shop. She knew she needed to talk to someone right away, someone who would understand and be sympathetic, but Luke was at work and wouldn't be over to her house until later in the evening. Her mother was definitely out of the question, and so was Trina—they would probably side with Elwin. Laura. That's who she needed to see.

They had been best friends all through high school and had shared each other's triumphs and failures. Cassie had been much closer to Laura than to her own sister. But when Cassie went away to college and Laura got married, they began to drift apart. They wrote one another often, but their diverging lifestyles and interests seemed to weaken the bond. Then Cassie returned to Plymouth and the closeness they'd once had began to rebuild.

Laura lived in a part of town that was aging poorly. Too old to be modern and too new to be gracious and stately, the boxy little houses marched like peas in a pod beneath medium-sized trees. Cassie drove to the fourth house from the corner and parked on the street; the drive was full of various tricycles and skateboards.

She mounted the steps and, reaching over a jumble of love-worn dolls set up for a tea party, rang the bell.

The door opened and Laura smiled a greeting. Her straight blond hair was slicked back in a ponytail, and she wore jeans and a tee shirt that read "Mr. Bill Lives." Motioning for Cassie to step over the dolls, she called out, "Janie, come clear off the porch. I told you not to leave your dolls outside." She looked out to Cassie's brand-new car parked at the curb but pretended not to notice. To Cassie, she said, "Come on back to the kitchen. I'm making formula and can't stop right now. I ran out of bottles and Timothy will wake up any time now."

Cassie followed her through the cluttered but cozy room to the kitchen. A smaller copy of Laura and two young boys sat eating cookies and milk at the kitchen table. "Hello, Janie, Tommy, Mark," Cassie greeted Laura's children. "Where's Kathy?"

"She's taking a nap, too, thank goodness," Laura answered, moving to an array of baby bottles on the worn cabinet. "I think she's coming down with a cold. Mark, don't do that to your cookie!" She glanced at Cassie, then nodded toward a chair. "How's your social life going? Met any good-looking hunks lately?" They hadn't talked since Cassie told Laura she had won the lottery.

Cassie found herself blushing. "Actually, I have. His name is Luke Bennett and he designs space suits."

"For a living, you mean? I didn't know anyone did that. Tommy, don't blow bubbles in your milk. Mark, I told you to stop it!"

"I want you to meet him. He's really wonderful."

"So why the long face?" Laura gave her oldest son a withering look and pointed at him warningly.

"I lost my job. Oh, Laura, it was just awful. Ever since I won the lottery, people have been calling me, begging for money, even demanding it! They call me at home, at work, they collar me at parties. They actually come to the shop."

"Oh?" Laura gave her a compassionate glance, then said, "Janie, you do that once more and I'm going to spank you! I'm sorry, Cassie, what were you saying?"

"The worst of the lot showed up today. He was really spooky. He kept talking about the end of the world and scars on thumbs. I got rid of him, but Elwin had had enough and he fired me right there in front of Bill and Ilene Goodrow."

"He fired you?"

"Yes! Now what will I do? You know how much I liked that job. Elwin is kind of dingy, but I really enjoyed working with the flowers."

"A lot of people are getting laid off. My Tom thinks he may be at any time. At least you don't need the money."

"That money has been the cause of more trouble than it has good! Because of it, I've lost my job, Mom and Trina were cool to me for days, and my life is a fishbowl. I can't buy groceries without a reporter asking me how it feels to be rich overnight."

"At least you can buy groceries," Laura said tightly. "If Tom's laid off, I don't know what we'll do." She reached past Cassie and swatted Janie, who was about to stuff cookie crumbs up her nose. An offended wail split the air.

"I'm sorry, Laura. I didn't think of that," Cassie

called out contritely over Janie's shrieks. "Can I help? I'll loan you whatever you need."

Laura glared at her. "I don't take charity." A toddler appeared at the door, rubbing her eyes and sobbing hoarsely. Laura took one look at the bright pink cheeks and glazed eyes and diagnosed, "Fever. I knew Kathy was sleeping too soundly." She swooped the little girl up and tried to smooth the fine blond hair. "She's burning up."

"Can I hold her?" Cassie asked, offering her hands.

"No, she gets cranky when she doesn't feel well." The child confirmed this by burying her face against Laura's throat, clinging tightly and raising her sobs an octave.

"Laura, please let me help," Cassie implored. She pushed Janie's milk closer to distract her, then caught Mark's hand as he aimed a blow at his brother. "What good is all that money if I can't use it to help my friend?"

"Damn! I see Timothy awake in there," Laura moaned as she peered across the hall. "What good is it! I really wouldn't know, Cassie. I have my hands full with just day-to-day living. I don't have time to ponder the problems of having seven million dollars dumped in my lap."

Cassie's eyes widened at Laura's angry words. "I didn't mean to—"

"Maybe you'd better go," Laura snapped as Kathy's howls increased and Tommy swung back at Mark. "I really don't have time to visit today."

"I'm trying to help!" Cassie objected.

"I can't work up much sympathy for you at the

moment. Maybe if you had some *real* problems, you could solve the easy ones like a tiff with Elwin."

Cassie bit back her retort. "I'm sorry I bothered you," she said stiffly.

Laura nodded but turned away, jiggling Kathy in a futile effort to stop her sobs.

Stinging from Laura's rejection, Cassie found her own way out. After the cacophony inside, the outside calm was a welcome contrast. Now she had yet another mark on the minus side of her fortune. The money had caused a rift between her and her best friend. It did no good to tell herself Laura was both overworked and overworried. Cassie had seen that same hostile expression on several people in the past few days.

Numbly, she went down the cement walk to her car. At least, she tried to reassure herself as she drove home, she still had Luke. Or did she?

She parked in the garage and crossed her shady lawn. Her feet made shuffling noises in the red and gold leaves that hid the grass. Above her the trees domed in brilliant foliage. She absently fished a handful of leaves from the basin of the fountain and walked between the privet hedges to the gap in the trees that led to her private section of beach.

Maybe, she thought dismally, she didn't have Luke at all. She hadn't known him before she won the lottery, except for those few hours. Perhaps he was dating her only because of her money. That would certainly explain why he was so personally attentive when men usually treated her as a buddy or even a kid sister. Cassie didn't put much stock in her sex appeal, since she wasn't sure she had any. Quite probably, she decided, she would never have heard from Luke after that first date if she were still merely Cassie Collins who worked in the Daisy Dilly Flower Shoppe.

With her head tilted even lower, Cassie continued on the path down a shallow hill to the strip of pale beach. A breeze was blowing in from the sea and the waves were whispering their endless secrets to the sand. Cassie zipped her pale green jacket and jammed her hands down in her pockets. She couldn't bear the thought that Luke might be more interested in her money than in her, yet she was much too honest to deny the possibility.

The wind caught her dark hair and tossed it about as she wandered along the beach. She often came here with her problems; her Aunt Cassandra had teased her about Neptune being her analyst. Cassie wished her aunt were around now to tell her what to think about Luke. She turned automatically at the edge of her property and began retracing her footprints in the soft sand. Her attention was so distracted that she jumped when she heard Luke's voice.

"I didn't see you," she exclaimed. Her heart was fluttering in her chest like a trapped butterfly, but she wasn't sure whether that was because she had been startled or because of Luke's nearness. Protectively, she concluded that it was the former.

"That's how I get beautiful women to talk to me," he said with a grin. "I sneak up on them."

"Aren't you early?"

"Yes. Do you mind?"

"Why do you want to date me?" she asked bluntly.

He glanced at her, then looked out to sea as if the answer might be riding the crest of one of the waves. "I want to date you because you've got an infectious laugh, a funny dimple on one cheek, and my conversations with you are the strangest I've ever had."

"That's it?" she grilled him. If he so much as mentioned the money, she was going to push him into the sea and never date him again.

He turned his attention entirely on her, and his eyes were as green as the calm water beyond the breakers. "That and the fact that I love you."

Cassie's breath caught in her throat. Had she misunderstood him? "What did you say?" she gasped.

"I said I love you. I know this may seem sudden to you and I guess I shouldn't have said anything yet, but you're all I can think about."

It did seem sudden to Cassie. Too sudden. She had to know. "Do you love me because of my money?"

A little chuckle escaped his lips before he answered, "I love you in spite of it." He waited quietly as the waves tumbled and a gull called overhead. When she just stood there looking stunned, he added, "I hadn't planned to tell you like this. I wanted moonlight in a garden of roses with an orchestra playing in the background. But roses are out of season and orchestras cost a bundle."

"I hear there will be moonlight tonight," she said, finding her tongue at last. "One out of three isn't bad." Her doubts were ebbing as she studied the depths of his eyes and found no indication of deception.

He sighed and looked back out beyond the waves.

"I shouldn't have done it like this. It's just that you look so—I don't know. There's just something about you that makes me want to put my arms around you and protect you, yet at the same time I want you to stand beside me and square off at the world. Does that make sense?"

Cassie nodded and reached out to touch the nubby weave of his sweater. "I love you, too."

His head snapped back to face her. "You do?"

Wordlessly she nodded. Suddenly his arms were around her and he was whirling her about in the air. Cassie held tightly to him. When he stopped spinning, he let her slide down his body until her feet touched the sand. No words were needed as they gazed into each other's souls. Whole universes were mirrored in their eyes.

"I never expected it to be like this," Luke said at last as he stroked her hair back from her face.

Here it comes, Cassie thought, the part where he says he originally felt I would make a good buddy and then fell in love with me by accident. She braced herself.

"You're so much more wonderful than I ever expected you'd be."

Caught off-balance, Cassie said apologetically, "I'm not a sexy blonde."

"No, you're a sexy brunette."

"Men prefer blondes."

"Only in old movies. I like brunettes."

Cassie smiled. The relief made her limp. "I'm glad I had the good sense to fall in love with you."

Slowly Luke lowered his head and kissed her. She curved toward him and ran her tongue over his lips, tasting the sea's saltiness. Her heart quickened as his tongue met hers and smoothed over the tender inner curve of her lips. The world vanished, and all that was left in her universe was Luke and the love singing throughout her being.

When he at last pulled back, he said, "I think we'd better go inside before we draw a crowd."

"I can't stop kissing you long enough to go inside," she murmured against his lips.

"We'll take it by stages." He led her up the hill and paused beneath the golden poplar. Again his lips found hers, and he sighed appreciatively when she molded her body to his.

At the fountain they stopped again. This time Cassie pulled his head down and tiptoed up to kiss him. When she released him, he said huskily, "Lady, you're almost too good to be true!"

Two more kisses took them to the back door. "Maybe we ought to stay out here," he said, pulling her into his arms. "I want to do a whole lot more than just kiss you."

Cassie stood on the step so that their eyes were level. With a gentle smile she said, "I know. I want you, too."

"You're sure?" His large hands moved up and down her back, feeling her delicate form and drawing her closer.

"I was sure last night. I'm even more positive today."

"I sure wish you had mentioned that last night." He grinned as his forehead met hers. "We both might have slept better."

Cassie took his hand and led him through the enclosed porch and the kitchen to the stairway. Suddenly shyness assailed her and she stopped.

"What's wrong?" he asked. "Having second thoughts?"

"No." She looked up at him and took a deep breath. "Luke, I'm not very experienced."

This wasn't what he had expected her to say. "Is this your first time?"

"No," she answered, "but it almost is. I'm afraid I won't please you."

"Cassie, I love you. I want to hold you and caress you and love you. I'm not going to grade you. But if your kisses are any indication, you're going to please me a great deal."

"I don't think so," she said in a burst of honesty. "I don't seem to ever quite . . . turn on." A fiery blush colored her cheeks and her eyes avoided his.

Luke smiled. "Let's see if I can change that. I want you to enjoy this as much as I'm sure I will."

She managed to return his smile, but she climbed the stairs slowly. She knew what she was talking about and she wasn't exaggerating. True, his kisses filled her with fire, but that was no sign her lovemaking would satisfy him.

Her bedroom was on the east side of the house, overlooking the water. A large bay window, though covered with old-fashioned lace curtains for privacy, admitted a good deal of light. Her bed was an oak four-poster, highly polished from generations of use. A matching chifforobe stood against the wall, and a plump chair upholstered in peach and green sat by a side table and lamp. No man had been to this room with her before, and she glanced at him nervously.

Sensing her shyness, Luke took her in his arms and held her securely until she relaxed against him. Then he put his forefinger under her chin and lifted her face for his kiss. Gently he claimed her lips and felt them open in welcome. She was so delicate in his arms, and so responsive. Yet her shyness was almost a fear, and he wondered if this was due to her earlier experiences. While he had no Victorian desire that the woman he loved be a virgin, and although he knew he would never ask her, he was curious whether her timidity was because of some insensitive lover. He hoped it wasn't, because she deserved better than that.

Moving gently so as not to alarm her, Luke unzipped her jacket and brushed it off her shoulders. "Cassie, you're awfully quiet. Are you afraid? If you've changed your mind, I'll understand."

She shook her head, her eyes large and dark. "I haven't changed my mind."

"If you do, at any time, tell me. I want it to be good for you."

She nodded. Her fingers were cold and her palms were sweaty. She hoped he wouldn't notice. When he kissed her again, her heart pounded so hard it would have frightened her if it hadn't felt so right.

Realizing he was waiting for her to make the first move, Cassie slipped her hands under his sweater and pulled it up and over his head. Running her hands over his bare chest, she caught her breath. Not only was he incredibly handsome, but he had a body to match. Although this excited her, it also caused her a flutter of trepidation. She wasn't at all sure her own was pretty enough.

Luke unbuttoned her blouse and slid it off her shoulders. Absently Cassie gave thanks to her mother's insistent instruction that she should always wear nice underwear, in case of an accident; but Cassie was certain no doctor would ever have examined her bra the way Luke was.

He unbuttoned the opening of her skirt, then brushed it and her half-slip down to pool around her ankles. She stood there almost defiantly in her barely concealing bra and bikini panties, watching to see his reaction.

"You're the most beautiful sight I've ever seen," he said at last. His fingers found the catch of her sheer bra and he pulled it free, baring her full breasts to his gaze. "You're perfect," he breathed.

Relief flooded over her. Cassie fumbled with the waistband of his jeans, and soon he stood naked before her. Every inch of him was as gorgeous as she had thought it might be. "You look as if you came straight from Mount Olympus," she murmured. "Nobody ought to look this terrific."

"I love you," he said gently, his eyes loving hers. Even though he wanted to drink in the luscious vision of her body, he wanted more to put her at ease.

She swayed into his arms, her turgid nipples brushing against his chest. "I love you, Luke."

He bent to lift her in his embrace and carried her to

the bed. He put her down gently, then sat beside her to gaze at her long and sensuously before pulling aside the covers and pressing her back onto the mattress.

Cassie lay back, and he rolled over her to lie beside her. Again he kissed her, and only then did he let his hand move over her side to caress her breast. Cassie's arms tightened instinctively. She loved lying in Luke's arms and feeling the firmness of his body against hers, but she felt no more urgency to join with him than she had expected.

Luke smoothed his hand over the warm fullness of her breast and caressed her rosy nipple with his open palm. She kissed his neck and nuzzled in the curve between his throat and shoulder until he thought he would explode from wanting her. But still her body lay quietly beside him, and he schooled himself to patience.

Lowering his head, he kissed the pliant flesh beneath his hand. "You smell so good," he breathed. "And your skin is as smooth as satin." Cassie ran her fingers through his hair and tried hard to summon passion. His fingers ran beneath the waistband of her panties and eased them lower. Obligingly, she rolled so that he could pull them away. Now, she knew, he would pull her beneath him and enjoy her. Almost frantically, she tried to become excited before it was too late.

But instead, he merely stroked her hip and murmured love words against her breast. To her surprise, he kissed her again and again until his mouth found her nipple, which he took between his lips. His hot tongue laved it, and she felt the tiniest spark of response leap to life in the center of her being. Taking his time, Luke loved first one breast, then the other.

Hardly daring to move lest he stop what he was doing, Cassie let her head roll back and found her body was arching naturally to give him better access to her breasts. A thrill ran through her, and she moaned softly as he brought her nipples to throbbing urgency with his fingers as well as with his lips and tongue.

Only when she moved restlessly did his hand glide lower to stroke the nest of curls above her thighs. Now, she knew, he would take her, and she braced herself for the discomfort. Instead, he only stroked her, urging her thighs to part but not insisting that they should.

Willingly she opened herself to him, and his fingers discovered her most secret parts. Pleasure flooded over Cassie, and she sighed happily as she felt herself grow ready for his loving.

Still his lips and tongue teased her breasts, and Cassie's ardor intensified as his fingers quickened her womanhood. Never had she experienced an urgency such as was thundering through her. Love for Luke became the wellspring of her existence as she blossomed beneath his knowing touch.

When she thought she would faint from wanting more of his love, she found the words upon her lips, urging him to become one with her, murmuring of her love for him. Only then did he join his body with hers.

There was no discomfort. Their bodies met and merged with a rightness that took away her breath. When he began to move and to whisper the words of love her soul hungered for, Cassie joined him smoothly in love's rhythm. A fiery light grew within her until it encompassed them both and Cassie felt a soaring, a spiraling upward that she had never known before. As she reached love's peak, she cried out in abandoned ecstasy and heard him do the same as wave after thundering wave washed through her.

Gradually the need melted into pure, warm pleasure and she had the curious sensation of floating with Luke through a golden cloud. Her lips echoed her total contentment and she snuggled deeper into his embrace. "I never knew it could be like this," she sighed. "I never dreamed it could be so good."

His arms tightened lovingly and he kissed her damp forehead. "I guess that's the difference love makes," he said in an awed voice. "I never felt anything quite like that either."

Cassie nodded agreeably, but she was pretty sure her revelation had been a lot more surprising than his. She let the golden cloud lull her to sleep in Luke's arms as the rolling sea beyond her window echoed her earlier passion.

5

The next day dawned cloudy and by midmorning an intermittent drizzle had become a soaking rain. The gaily bedecked autumn trees bowed under the water's weight, and the sea flattened into a milky shade of slate. The steady plop of raindrops was augmented by an occasional birdcall.

Cassie lit the heater on the glassed-in porch, and she and Luke sat cuddled together on the pillow-strewn daybed watching the rain. She wore snug jeans and a bulky sweater of muted lavender and blue.

"More coffee?" Luke asked as he poured himself another cup from the percolator.

"No, thanks." She curled her fingers around her warm cup and sipped the steaming liquid. "I never knew anything could be so perfect," she sighed dreamily. "A pot of coffee, rain outside with us snug inside, and most of all, you."

". . . beside me singing in the wilderness," Luke quoted.

With a laugh, Cassie laid her head on his shoulder. "There hasn't been a wilderness around here in hundreds of years. You do bring out the primitive in me, however."

"I remember," he said, grinning. "I'm surprised you didn't want to sleep late. We didn't get much rest last night." He kissed the soft tendrils curling on her forehead.

"I can't sleep. I'm more alive than I ever have been before. If it weren't raining I'd be out there in the yard running in circles, I feel so full of life." She gazed up at him. "Do you feel that way, too?"

He nodded and his eyes softened. "I sure do, honey." The Southern endearment rolled warmly off his tongue.

Cassie smiled contentedly. Coming from Luke, the term made her feel loved and cherished beyond measure. "What's North Carolina like? When you talk I hear magnolias in your voice."

"It's beautiful. I grew up in a house very similar to this one, only made of red brick. We had a big yard, too, full of those magnolias and camellias. My mother's hobby is gardening and my father's is avoiding gardening, so I got to see a lot of that yard. I'll show it to you someday."

After a pause, Cassie said, "You want me to meet your parents?"

"Of course I do." He looked sideways at her. "Why wouldn't I?"

"I wasn't sure you wanted me in your life to that extent."

"You have a very short memory. I told you I love you. We spent most of the night demonstrating it. Remember?"

"'I love you' doesn't necessarily mean the same thing to everybody."

Luke pulled her closer and lay his cheek against her hair. "When I say it, I mean it. In the old-fashioned way. Those aren't words to take lightly. What about you?"

Cassie smiled and the dimple appeared on her cheek. "I'm old-fashioned, too." Then she asked with feigned nonchalance, "Are you going to see Maureen again?"

"Absolutely not. How about you?"

"I'll have nothing to do with her," Cassie promised solemnly, a twinkle lighting her eyes.

"You know what I mean. Any boyfriends lurking in the wings?"

"Not a one. I don't want any man but you." Cassie looked away and concentrated her gaze on the rain. Her words sounded more like a proposal than she had intended. Love was one thing, but marriage was permanent—at least in her view. To change the subject, she said, "I'm so glad you didn't belittle my losing my job. On top of the argument with Laura and the strain I've been under, it would have been too much."

"Getting fired is no light matter." He still couldn't

see why this Laura person hadn't been more considerate. "Do you think he'll hire you back?"

"No. He's been looking for an excuse to let me go ever since I won the lottery. I never dreamed seven million dollars came with twice as many problems." She rubbed her head against his cheek. "I'm glad the money isn't driving you away."

"That doesn't seem to be a sensible reason for leaving," he said with a grin. Seeing her smile waver, he added, "Have you decided what to do with the money?"

"I've thought of opening my own flower shop. I know flowers and I enjoy working with them."

"You and my mother are going to get along great," Luke said. "I can see you two now, laying out flower beds on every visit." He drank his coffee and listened to the low rumble of thunder before he said, "Do you have a place in mind for your shop?"

"Not really. I'd like for it to be near the sea. Maybe in one of those refurbished houses the city zoned for commercial use recently. There're several small ones with large windows to let in sunlight. And I'm *not,*" she vowed, "going to make any employee wear a red plastic apron with *Daisy Dilly* written in flowers on the front!"

"How about *Pilgrim's Posies?*" he teased. "Or *May Flowers?*"

"How about a punch in the nose?" she countered.

"Seriously, I think a flower shop is a good idea. If you want my help, just let me know. I don't know a violet from a rubber plant, but I can move heavy pots and paint walls."

"You'd do that?"

"Sure, I would."

"You really must love me," she said happily. "I may just take you up on that. I think I'll go to a real estate office Monday and see what's available."

"What are you going go do this afternoon?"

"I told Trina I'd go over to her house. It's her birthday, but I'm not supposed to tell anyone. She's decided to keep them secret now. That's why I can't ask you to come along. Mom and I are going to meet over there, celebrate quietly, then slip away. Personally, I think she's being silly. I don't see any big deal about getting older—everyone does if they live out the year."

Luke smiled. He was secretly glad not to be included in Trina's birthday plans. Although he had seen her only once, he knew he would never learn to like her.

"I have a plan," Cassie continued blithely. "When I get a little older, I'm going to tell people I'm older than I really am. Then they'll be impressed that someone that old can look so young. What do you think?"

"Interesting idea. I want to see it in action."

"You will." Cassie realized she had just assumed Luke would be here years in the future. She would have to watch herself. Luke hadn't said a word about marriage, and he might never.

"Will you be home by dinner?"

"Yes. Trina and Dick—that's her husband—are going out tonight."

"It sounds pretty elaborate for a secret celebration."

"She means no more birthday parties. However, she didn't say not to bring a gift," Cassie chuckled.

"Do you two get along well?" Somehow he couldn't imagine their having a very close relationship.

"Not necessarily. Trina is older than I am by a number of years. We were more like two only children than sisters. All my life Trina has been my other mother, and no girl needs two. She's always giving me advice whether it's asked for or not. The galling thing is that sometimes she's right. And when she is, she gloats."

"Then why go see her?"

"I feel sorry for her. Dick is out of town more often than he's home, and they don't have a strong marriage. Mom doesn't know, but I think Trina and Dick are about to separate. I want her to know she has me to lean on if she needs me. She has very few friends."

"It doesn't sound as though she'd do the same for you if the tables were turned. I mean, she didn't even seem happy for you the day you won the lottery."

"I don't blame her for her reaction. That's just the way Trina is. At any rate, she's predictable."

"Of course that's your business, but I have a hard time with the thought that anyone might hurt your feelings or take advantage of you. You're just too important to me."

Cassie settled more comfortably in the warm circle of his arm and wondered if any woman had ever been this much in love.

"Happy birthday," Cassie said in a stage whisper as she handed Trina her gift.

"Don't remind me," her sister moaned. But she took the gift and started to unwrap it.

"Nonsense. I wouldn't overlook your birthday or you might forget mine," she quipped.

"It won't be long before you'll be hoping everyone does. You just don't know."

Cassie's smile wavered but she held tightly to her good mood. She was no stranger to Trina's depressions.

Trina opened the box and took out a purse woven in warm desert colors. "How lovely." Her voice sounded slightly disappointed, but she smiled. "Do you think it's too young for me?"

"Of course not. I think it will be perfect with your beige pantsuit and that pumpkin-colored silk blouse Mom gave you for Christmas." Too late, Cassie realized Trina must have expected a more expensive gift in view of her windfall. "It's handwoven and the fabric is colored with vegetable dye. I think I may get one for myself before they're sold out."

"It's darling, but don't buy one. I'll loan you mine."

Trina had done it again. She had managed to turn a gesture of sharing into an insult. But rather than being thin-skinned and getting upset, Cassie changed the subject. "Has Mom been over yet?"

"No. She called and said she would come later." Trina held the purse up again, turned it around in a critical observation and set it back in the box.

"Did Dick give you a gift yet?"

"Honestly, Cassie, you make too big a deal out of birthdays. He suggested I go out and buy whatever I want. It's much more logical when you think about it.

He never chooses anything I want and I just have to exchange it."

"I was hoping things were better between you two."

"There's not much chance of that."

Trina took a cigarette from the packet in her purse and lit it. "We've decided to give ourselves until Christmas to try to work it out."

"That's not very long. Have you been to a marriage counselor?"

"Dick won't go. And really, I don't see any reason to air our problems in public. The trouble started between us, and that's where it has to be worked out."

"What are you doing to change things?" Cassie probed.

"Really! You ask the most personal questions." Trina blew smoke up over her head in an indignant gesture. "I'm going shopping later. Would you like to go? Since Dick told me to buy my own gift, I think I'll get a fur. My old one is so out of style. If the marriage breaks up, I may as well get as much as I can out of it."

Cassie looked thoughtfully at Trina. "How do you suppose Mom and Dad had such different children? You and I are nothing alike."

Trina shrugged. "I'm like Mom and you're like Dad."

"Do you remember the party you had on your twelfth birthday? We went to the park, and Mom had even hired a clown."

"Yes, I do. You rode the whirl-around too many times and threw up."

"I had forgotten about that."

"It was a long time ago. So many years."

"For goodness' sake, Trina! You sound as if you're on your last leg. Snap out of it!" Cassie could take only so much self-pity.

Trina ground out her half-finished cigarette. "What have you been up to lately?"

"I've been thinking of opening up my own flower shop." She hadn't told Trina about being fired.

"That's a good idea. I just detest that Daisy Dilly shop. It's simply too cutesy for my taste. You know what you should do? Get one of those spaces in that new shopping center that's being built west of town and specialize. Sell only orchids or just roses. The secret is to build a reputation—be unique."

"I'm not sure that's such a good idea," Cassie said doubtfully. "A florist shop relies on many customers, all with different tastes."

"Don't listen to me then, but you're wrong. Just think of banks and banks of orchids."

"Orchids aren't right for every occasion. You wouldn't send a bouquet of orchids to a hospital room."

"Why not? Be innovative."

Cassie glanced at the chrome and glass clock on the wall and wondered if she could leave yet.

Trina reached for another cigarette. "Are you still seeing that redheaded man?"

"Luke? Yes, but his hair is auburn, not red."

"Same thing, really. Cassie, I know you don't like advice, but I have to say this for your own good."

Cassie felt her insides start to shrivel. "I have to go now."

"Hear me out first." Trina put a restraining hand on Cassie's arm. "Have you considered that he might be . . . well, more interested in your money than in you?"

"Trina!"

"It's not that you aren't attractive, dear, but it *is* rather coincidental, isn't it? I mean, you never saw him until you won the money."

"I met him before I won it," Cassie protested. "At least, it was a few hours before I got the call."

"That's not very long, is it?"

"No, but that doesn't matter."

"Do you two go out often?"

"Very often. Almost every night."

Trina's big blue eyes grew moist with sympathy. "And that doesn't strike you as odd?"

"It strikes me as wonderful."

"All right. Have it your own way." Trina held her hands up in a gesture of surrender and shook her head. "But don't come running to me when he breaks your heart."

"I have to go. I really do." Cassie stood abruptly and pulled on her coat. "Happy birthday."

"What a shame you have to rush off. We so seldom get a chance to talk."

"Yes, well, give Terry my love and tell him I'll be by tomorrow to take him to the park. If it's all right with you."

"He'd love it. You're so good with children. Around here he's a holy terror."

Cassie suppressed a smile. Terry had tried to treat her that way, too, but she had put a stop to it. Now he was well behaved when he came to visit her. "Tell Dick I said hello."

"All right."

Cassie hurried out and walked briskly to her car. Trina was always full of bad tidings, she reminded herself, always ready to spread gloom and doom. What she had suggested about Luke was nonsense. Sure, the thought had occurred to her and she had wondered about it, but when she asked Luke, he had assured her it was not the money. Suddenly, doubt clouded Cassie's thoughts. The first time he told her he loved her was the same day she'd asked him about the money. Did Luke really love her?

She drove to the nearest phone booth and dialed his number. When he answered, she said, "Luke? This is Cassie. Say, I was wondering what you would think about me giving a very large donation to charity."

"It's your money," his voice replied.

Cassie drew a deep breath and gripped the phone. "I was thinking about giving all of it away."

"*All* of it?" he gasped. "Cassie, why would you want to do that?"

"You would mind, then?"

"What I think about it isn't important, but a person doesn't just give away seven million dollars! You don't even have a job!"

"Okay. I just wondered what you would think about the idea. I'll see you later. Bye." She hung up but continued to stare at the phone. Trina might be right after all.

Luke replaced the receiver in its cradle and frowned down at the phone. Was someone trying to pressure Cassie out of her money? That many millions could turn heads. He went back to his small kitchen and pushed up the sleeves of his gray sweat shirt before again attacking the sinkful of dishes.

Hands in the sudsy water, Luke stared out his window into the tiny private courtyard. A person didn't give away seven million dollars! Not if that was all she had and she had even lost her job. It didn't make sense at all.

Still frowning, Luke flicked most of the soap off his hands and dried his palms on his jeans as he went back to the telephone. He punched out Cassie's number and waited. Long rings reverberated metallically in his ear as a ribbon of soap bubbles slipped over his wrist. Finally he hung up and glared at the phone. Where could she have called from?

Because he didn't know what else to do, Luke went back to the dishes. He slowly washed a plate, running the sponge over the slick surface as one scenario after another played in his mind. "I'll bet some shyster is trying to put one over on her," he muttered to himself.

He rinsed the plate and stuck it in the drainer with the glass and the coffee cup. With only himself to clean up after, he rarely used the dishwasher. "I'd better get over there." When he realized he was talking to himself, his jaw slammed shut and he shook his head.

Cassie's eccentricities were already rubbing off on him. With a brief smile at the thought, he let the water drain and then, using the kitchen towel, wiped the soapsuds from his hands.

All the way to Cassie's house, Luke worried about her. Now that he thought about it, she had sounded upset. Her voice had had that husky sound it got when she was trying to sound cheerful but felt sad. Something had definitely upset her. But what?

Luke parked and went to ring the doorbell. A cold wind was whistling off the waves, and he hunched his shoulders and zipped his jacket up under his chin. Again he rang the bell.

After waiting long enough for her to get there from the furthest reaches of the house, he went around back and knocked on the back door. When she still didn't answer, he tried the knob. It turned in his hand.

Dread pierced him. No one he knew left his house unlocked. Maybe she had met with a criminal. Had she been trying to say something between the lines when she called? But that made no sense.

He went in and stood uncertainly in the kitchen. "Cassie?" he called. Then, more loudly, "Cassie, are you home?"

With trepidation, Luke searched through the house. His concern grew as he went upstairs and, after pausing for a second, shoved against her bedroom door. With a bang, the door slammed against the wall, causing him to jump; but this room was as empty as the others had been. Luke ran his fingers through his hair and peered around the room. Where was she?

He went back downstairs and was heading into the

kitchen when the swinging door thudded against something solid on the other side. He heard a yelp of surprise. "Cassie?" he called out.

"Luke?" came the frightened reply.

He pushed the door open slowly and saw Cassie standing there wide-eyed. "Are you all right?" he asked too loudly.

"Of course I am. What are you doing here?"

As his anxiety left him, he found himself snapping at her in his relief at finding her safe. "Don't you know not to leave your house unlocked? Somebody could just walk in!"

"Obviously."

He didn't notice her sarcasm. "What was that nonsense about giving away all your money? You didn't, did you?"

"No."

"Thank goodness! Look, if you want me to help you find ways to invest it, I will. All you have to do is say so. But don't, for heaven's sake, throw it away."

Cassie stared at him. With every word he said, her doubts grew stronger. "I wasn't going to throw it away."

"Most people would give anything to have that kind of money. You don't seem to realize that."

"Yes, I'm afraid I do." She felt a sickening sensation spread from the pit of her stomach. Was he confirming Trina's theory that he was only after her money? "I only wondered if you thought it would be a good idea. After all, it's causing me a lot of trouble."

"Everyone should have that trouble." He grinned to relieve the tension, and put his arms around her.

"Honey, just promise me you won't do anything foolish."

"Foolish!" She pushed against him but he held her close.

"All right, not foolish. But don't do anything without thinking it through."

"Without asking you, you mean?"

"I'll be more than happy to give you my advice."

"Thanks, but I have more than enough people advising me already."

"Hey, I didn't mean to upset you. What's going on here?" He looked deeply into her troubled brown eyes. "Cassie?"

She shook her head and sighed before burying her face against his chest. "Don't pay me any attention, Luke. I guess I'm just not myself right now."

He held her securely. "That's okay, honey. You can't be up all the time."

Cassie clung to him, wishing she had mailed Trina's gift to her instead of delivering it in person. Now she was assailed with doubts. "I love you," she murmured miserably.

"I love you, too." He was glad everything was all right now.

6

"Have you got everything?" Cassie asked Luke for the twentieth time.

"I think so. Did you remember your camera?"

"It's in this bag. Isn't this exciting?" Cassie bubbled as she looked around the crowded terminal. A professionally polite voice announced that flight 501 for Los Angeles was boarding at gate 3. "That's us." She nervously thrust her hair behind her ear and shouldered the nylon webbed strap of her flight bag.

The decision to rush off to Los Angeles on the spur of the moment had truly been an inspiration. She had struggled for days with the notion that Luke might be more interested in her money than in her, and she figured that this spending spree would give her a chance to observe his reaction to some genuinely extravagant behavior. And, too, she wanted to go, simply because she could.

"I still say this is the strangest date I've ever had," Luke commented as they got in line to board the plane.

"It was my time to treat you. Ever since we started dating, you've picked up the tab."

"I never picked one up this big," he reminded her. "I still don't feel comfortable doing this."

"Don't start that again. You agreed to go wherever I wanted to go on my date."

"But to California? I expected something like a nice restaurant or maybe a dinner theater."

"I've been to those places. I've never seen the Pacific Ocean."

"Most people go to the beach in the summer."

"That's months away. Besides, this is when you had some time off work. We'll miss the crowd this way."

"Lady, you're nuts," Luke joked affectionately.

"I know, and I sure am enjoying it." Cassie noted his resistance to her spending so much on a whim and was pleased that he seemed to feel that way. If he were interested in only her money, he would have been thrilled that she was willing to lavish so much of it on a good time for them both. Cassie decided it was okay to relax a bit and enjoy the trip.

They boarded the plane and found seats in the nonsmoking section. Cassie snapped her seat belt, did her usual wing check out the tiny window and adjusted the jet of air away from her eyes. Luke nonchalantly pulled a magazine from the seat pocket in front of him and was glancing at the articles.

The plane edged away from the boarding gate and taxied into position at the end of the runway. Cassie tensed and gripped the armrests. A roar filled the cabin and she was aware of the increase of pressure against her back as the huge plane hurtled forward.

"Are you nervous?" Luke asked over the noise.

"Yes!" she called back. "I hate to fly."

"Then why in the hell did you book us to fly all the way across country?" he exclaimed.

"I love to travel—only I hate flying."

"But—"

"It's too far to drive."

Shaking his head in amazement, Luke pried her fingers from the seat and held her hand. "Your fingers are like ice," he observed. "Relax. Everything's fine."

"I know." She spared him an unsteady smile and riveted her eyes straight ahead. "This isn't my first flight."

"You must want to see that ocean pretty badly."

"I do! All my life I've wanted to go to California."

The plane banked and began its ascent to cruising altitude. Luke, who was a seasoned traveler and loved flying, ordered Cassie a strong drink, saw to it that she drank it, and tried to put her at ease by showing her the beauty they were flying over. By the time they crossed the Rockies, Cassie was light-headed from both drink and excitement and was almost relaxed.

The landing was smooth, and Cassie felt triumphant as she preceded Luke off the plane. Los Angeles International Airport was a complex maze of boarding areas, escalators and shops. Cassie was thankful that Luke was familiar with the layout and was able to locate the baggage claim area with such ease.

Within an hour they had retrieved their luggage, rented a car, and were on their way out of town. Palm trees lined many of the streets, and beneath them were beds of flowers, still blooming in the mild weather.

"Did you remember to give Penny the key to your house?" Luke asked as he headed north on the Ventura Freeway.

"Yes, she always takes care of Phuzzbott and Mr. Beebles when I'm out of town. I sometimes think Phuzzbott prefers her; she brings him fresh catnip. Also, she's filling in for me at Crisis Hot Line. Damn! I'm not supposed to tell anyone I work there. Forget it, okay?"

He glanced over at her. "Is it a secret?"

She nodded. "We don't use our real names and it's supposed to be confidential who we are. That's to keep the callers from being able to reach us at home."

"I see." He exited the freeway and turned onto a narrow road. They crested a low rise and below them spread an endless expanse of blue-green water. "There it is. The Pacific Ocean. Was it worth the flight?"

"It's beautiful!" Cassie leaned forward eagerly as if by doing so she could reach the beach more quickly.

They drove along the curving beach road until their hotel came into view. Comprised of one multistoried building and numerous bungalows, the hotel complex sat in gracious luxury on a knoll beside a wide beach. Encircled by the ever-present palms, azaleas and grassy lawns, the buildings were white stucco topped with red Spanish tile. An enormous fluted fountain marked the main entrance, and a smaller replica lured visitors into the registration area.

Cassie followed Luke over the quarry-tiled foyer as Spanish music flowed softly through speakers hidden in banks of ivy and fern. They chose to stay in one of the bungalows rather than in the hotel proper and were assigned the one nearest the ocean.

Feeling as if she were living in a dream, Cassie took Luke's hand as they went down the curving, bark-strewn walk. The valet had already parked their car in the hotel's parking garage, and the bellman, who had hurried along ahead of them, had unlocked their door for them and deposited their luggage inside.

As Luke tipped the man, Cassie opened the wide curtains. Beyond, the waves crashed onto shore and withdrew for a fresh onslaught. "It's perfect!" Cassie marveled. "If anything, it's better than the travel agent described it."

Like the hotel, the small house was Spanish in design. The same type of quarry tiles that Cassie had seen in the hotel foyer floored the entry to their room and continued down the short hallway that led to the kitchenette and the bathroom. Beyond the tiled entry, a thick gold carpet spread over the sitting area and the bedroom. The couch and two chairs were tastefully upholstered in a blend of tan and chocolate corduroy. Better-than-average prints gave brilliance to the walls.

Luke caught her hand and pulled her toward the door. "Let's go see the water up close. Leave your shoes here."

"Wouldn't you rather get dressed for dinner? The

travel agent said this place is close to a restaurant called La Mansión. He said it's *very* exclusive," she added as a test.

"Right now, I'd rather see the beach up close with you."

With a broad smile, Cassie quickly kicked off her shoes as Luke did the same. In moments they were hurrying out the door and across the grass to the beach. After the cool grass, the sand was warm under Cassie's feet and she dug her toes in.

"I'll bet everyone is wearing a coat today back home," she chortled. "It's almost warm enough to swim here."

"Almost, nothing. We're going to."

"I didn't bring a suit! Who would have thought it would be this warm in late September?"

"You won't need a swimsuit."

"You mean go skinny-dipping? In public?" Her shocked tones made him grin.

"Look around. There's not a soul anywhere in sight. This late in the year we have the place to ourselves almost entirely."

"Us and a couple hundred staff members. As soon as I'd strip to the skin, I bet a dozen people would come by."

Luke thought a minute. "We'll wait until later. Once the sun goes down no one will see you."

They rolled up their pant legs and walked along the water's edge. Overhead, gulls swooped and shrieked in the cobalt sky. Offshore, a school of porpoises surfaced and rolled. Cassie and Luke vied to see who could find the largest and most perfect seashell.

"Here it is!" Cassie whooped, reaching down for her latest find. "The best shell on the beach." She stood and triumphantly showed it to Luke.

"Mine is larger."

"This one is more perfect. See? Yours is chipped and mine isn't. I won." She held it to her ear, though it was much too small to be a sound chamber. "I hear the ocean!"

"That *is* the ocean," Luke laughed. "I sure hope there's nothing living in that shell."

Cassie jerked it away from her ear and peered cautiously into the rosy curl. "It's empty. You're teasing me!"

She ran to the sea's edge and splashed water at Luke. He charged at her and with a pretended growl gathered her up in his arms and headed out to sea.

"Luke! Are you crazy?" Cassie laughed breathlessly. "Put me down!"

"Okay." He dropped her to her feet in the waist-deep water and steadied her as a billowing wave broke against her.

"Oh!" she gasped in surprise. "I didn't mean right here!" Before he could see what she was up to, Cassie jumped at him, letting the next wave give her momentum. He fell back with her on top of him and flailed helplessly until he could regain his footing.

Sputtering, he shook the water from his plastered hair. "I'll get you for that!"

With a playful shriek, Cassie plunged away, trying unsuccessfully to outrun him in the waves. Luke grabbed her, lifted her out of the water and tossed her into an oncoming wave.

Cassie lost her bearings for a moment as the wave rolled her over, but then she surfaced and swam back to Luke. Putting her arms around his neck, she wrapped her legs about his hips. "You win."

"What's the prize?"

"I am."

"All right!" He pressed his lips to hers in a full and very passionate kiss, tasting the salty tang of her willing mouth.

As the waves thrust against them, he ran his hands over the clinging fabric of her blouse. Beneath he could feel the luscious curves of her body. His pulse quickened in response as the water buoyed her rhythmically against him. The muscles in his loins tensed with her nearness.

"We seem to have added a whole new dimension to skinny-dipping," he observed as he leaned his forehead against hers. "You're fully clothed, and yet you're still the sexiest woman on the beach."

"I'm the *only* woman on the beach."

"A mere technicality." He kissed her again lightly. "Had enough swimming? I have."

"I'll race you to the bungalow!"

She released him and they ran hand in hand for the beach, stumbling and laughing like two children. Sand sprayed from beneath their feet, soon to be replaced by the thick grass, then the sun-warmed cement of the short walk in front of their door. Cassie was ahead, but before she could touch the door, Luke's long arm reached around her, and he cried out, "I won!"

"That's cheating! Your arms are longer than mine."

"It still counts."

"No, it doesn't."

Panting for breath, they leaned against the stuccoed wall. Luke finally said, "Okay, first one in the house wins."

They both shoved at the door and simultaneously jammed into the doorway in a tangle of arms and legs. That was obviously a tie, so Cassie yelled, "Last one to the bathtub loses!" Before the words were out of her mouth, she was sprinting over the tiles. "I won!" she announced.

"I let you!"

"You did not!" She threw her arms around his neck. "I like you," she told him. "You're my best friend."

"Oh, yeah? Well, that's good because you're my best friend, too." He kissed her on the end of her salty nose and tasted the grit of sand.

"One of the reasons I like you is because of the way you play with me. I guess I never will grow up—at least, I hope not."

"What's another reason?"

"I can outrun you."

"Saucy broad," he laughed as he swatted her on the buttocks. "Get out of those wet clothes."

"Who could resist a proposition phrased like that, you smooth-talking devil, you?" she teased, and the two of them fumbled out of their sodden clothes.

Luke turned on the shower and they stepped over the rim of the tub to rinse away the sand and sea. Luke unscrewed the cap on the shampoo the hotel had provided and poured a measure into his palm. Then to Cassie's delight, he rubbed it on her wet hair, lathering piles of bubbles into her sable tresses.

"I haven't had anyone wash my hair since I was a toddler," she said, luxuriating in the sensation. "This is great."

He rubbed her scalp, his large hands dwarfing her head. Cassie let her head roll back in sheer enjoyment. When he rinsed the lather away, she returned the favor by shampooing his hair.

"I never knew anyone with hair quite this color," she marveled. "At times it's dark red but sometimes it's almost as brown as mine."

"It's a family trait. Personally, I think it looks better on my sister."

"I don't know your sister, but I can tell you for sure I'll prefer it on you. And it's so thick!"

"Balding doesn't run in my family. I'll probably go straight to gray."

Cassie smiled up at him and saw the white lather making a cap on his head. "You'll look very distinguished in silver hair."

"Thanks, but I hope I have a while to go yet." He stuck his head under the stream of water and sluiced away the soap. Turning to the line of bottles arranged on the shelf in the shower, he said, "What else have we got here? Hah! Sit down."

"What?"

"I found some bubble bath." He flicked the lever to send water out of the spigot, then closed off the tub drain as he poured the crystals beneath the rushing water.

Cassie did as she was told, sitting down amid the growing mass of bubbles, the water from the tap flowing across her shoulders. Luke eased down opposite her, his legs intertwining with hers. As the bubbles rose higher, he cupped her chin and drew her face to his. His kiss was long and provocative, calling forth all her love.

She put her arms around his neck and kissed him again as the beading rivulets streamed down her arms and dripped from her elbows and nipples. "I love you," she murmured. "I love you more than I ever thought I could love anyone."

"I know, Cassie. I feel the same way about you. Every waking moment you're in my thoughts. At night I dream about you." He stroked her wet cheek as his eyes devoured her face.

"What do you dream?" she asked gently.

"At first I dreamed we were making love. Then you started appearing in unexpected places—you know how dreams are—and we would sit talking or walk off holding hands. One I recall very clearly. We had made love up in that big four-poster bed of yours. Then all of a sudden we were down on your beach just beyond your garden. I drew a big heart in the sand and we jumped in as if it were water. When we came up, I drew another one and we jumped into it, and so forth all the way down the beach like that."

"How lovely," she sighed. "I'm so glad I fell in love with you."

"So am I."

Luke reached behind her and turned off the water. Mounds of frothy bubbles surrounded them both. Only the foaming sound of bubbles forming and popping broke the silence. Luke gazed at her in rapturous wonder.

Her hair was sleek and nearly black against her head. Her eyes were dreamy, and dewy drops clung to her long, dark lashes. Against the white of the bubbles, her skin was a deep cream color, luminous with health. Water dripping off her hair ran in tiny rivulets across her slender shoulders and onto her perfectly shaped breasts, which rounded above the foam, their peaks rosy and pouting for his attention.

Luke touched her throat where her pulse hammered a strong, even rhythm, then let his fingers glide over her firm, slick flesh to the warm globe of her breast. A thin film of bubbles followed the trail of his fingers, floating over her apricot skin. Almost holding his breath in the face of her loveliness, Luke rolled the taut bud between his thumb and forefinger. Cassie's eyes closed in the sheer enjoyment of his caress, and her head tilted back on her graceful neck. Her nipple grew even tighter at his touch and deepened in hue to a ruddy coral.

His other hand mirrored his explorations and she murmured her delight. Luke had to struggle to hold himself in check. His desire for her was great, and only the certainty that they would both enjoy this much more if he waited prevented his rushing to the conclusion.

Moving with teasing slowness, he traced rapturous curlicues on the underside of her full breast and below the froth of bubbles to her flat stomach. Lovingly he encircled her navel, dipping his fingers into its silken recess. Cassie moaned and shifted her body so that she lay back against the sloping tub.

Luke's hands roamed lower to the soft nest of curls.

Gently he coaxed her to greater passion as he loved the petal softness of her womanhood.

Cassie's breath quickened as his fingers tempted and pleased her, and she reached for him in her desire. When her fingertips brushed the hard wall of his chest, he took her hand and kissed her palm while his other hand continued to stroke her.

"Let me love you," he murmured. "Let me give you this."

Cassie opened her eyes enough to see the love that shone on his face, and she smiled. All desire to move vanished from her as he probed and caressed her most sensitive area. She lay back and gave herself up to his care and loving.

The pace of her pulse quickened as his touch became more urgent, more insistent. Suddenly she was caught up in the ever-increasing rapture she had always found in his arms. She cried out and her breasts thrust upward as she reached her completion. At the same time, Luke's lips closed over one of her nipples, drawing it into the hot warmth of his mouth. She called his name as her body seemed to burst into golden spangles.

After a moment or two, when she could speak again, she smiled up into his loving face and asked, "Can we possibly make love in a bathtub?"

"If I could figure out a way, we would now."

Languorously she opened her eyes wider and her smile broadened. "Why is it that I never get enough of you?"

"I guess you're just in love."

"You're pretty good at guessing," she said as her

hands stroked his glossy skin. "Guess what I'm wanting to do now."

"I'd be cheating," he said as he smoothed her breasts and tested their weight in his palms. "I know exactly what you want to do."

He stood and flicked open the drain, then held out his hands to help her stand. Cassie let him pull her up, but she hesitated as she gazed over his body. "I see we want the same thing," she said admiringly.

They dried each other between kisses and caresses, then walked arm in arm to the bedroom. Cassie pulled back the covers and lay on the bed, rolling to give him room to join her. He eased down and brushed the pillows away as his body molded to hers.

"Damn, you feel good," he said hoarsely as she curved toward him. "You could drive a man mad."

"That's exactly what I have in mind," she promised seductively.

Starting at the warm hollow of his neck, Cassie licked butterfly nibbles over his skin. Pausing now and then to take his flesh gently between her teeth in a sexy parody of a bite, she worked her way over his chest. When she reached his nipples, she flicked the coppery circle with her moist tongue and grinned saucily at his answering moan.

Her hands stroked him, moving lower until she touched him in the way she had learned he loved. His eyes closed and muscles ridged his neck and stomach in his effort to control himself as she seductively caressed him.

Cassie glided her leg over his until she sat astride him, slowly, ever so slowly, uniting their bodies. A moan of pleasure escaped her parted lips and mingled with the sound he made in answer to her. For a moment she was still, enjoying the completeness of the sensation. Then she began to move in the sensuous rhythms of love.

Luke reached up and brushed her damp hair back from her face and shoulders. She was ravishing him with the sure guile of a born wanton, and he gloried in it. Knowing her shyness as he did, he knew this unabashed loving was clear proof of her trust and desire for him and him alone. The love he felt for her almost overwhelmed him, and he fought harder for control.

With passion-roughened fingers he stroked her thrusting breasts, teasing her nipples to aching tightness. Cassie braced her hands on his chest and leaned forward so he could fondle her more easily. Luke raised his head to taste her offered nipples and met her strokes with greater urgency.

All at once Cassie cried out in profound release and he felt her warmth ripple around him. The sensation triggered his own ecstasy and they flew from the summit together. Over and over they seemed to tumble in purest pleasure, their souls and minds merged, as well as their bodies.

A warm glow that seemed to originate in his loins spread throughout his body, wrapping him in total satisfaction. "I don't know how you feel about this," he murmured when he could again form words, "but I could learn to enjoy living like this."

He nuzzled her moist hair and breathed in the softly scented aroma of his Cassie. He wanted to continue, to ask her then and there to marry him, but he waited. To propose now might later be interpreted as mere passion talking. No, he told himself, he should wait until the right moment. Wait until she would know the words weren't ecstasy-induced. He smiled in satisfaction and again inhaled her scent.

Cassie curled against him and tried to corral her scattered thoughts. When they made love, she always found it difficult to focus on anything but the pleasures of his loving. She tried to understand the meaning behind his words. She was glad he liked her gift of a vacation, but did he mean he wanted to move here? Did he want to make a life of traveling and living in hotels? She was certainly enjoying herself, but her home was in Plymouth, not California.

Like an ugly stain, Trina's accusation that Luke wanted Cassie's money, not her, bled back into her mind.

Cassie frowned and shoved the thought away. He loved *her*. She knew he did! If he didn't, he wouldn't make love with her the way he did. He wouldn't—couldn't—look at her with his eyes mirroring the adoration of his soul. He couldn't!

But the truth was, Cassie had had very little experience in such matters and she wasn't positive. Closing her eyes tightly, she forced that thought away as well.

Luke, feeling her arms embrace him more tightly, took it as a signal of renewed passion. With a low chuckle he rolled over and claimed her lips in a long kiss that soon led to more loving.

7

Cassie and Luke walked hand in hand along the opalescent curve of beach. The swollen sun hung low on the horizon, turning the water to pearl and amethyst. The sky was a velvet dome of purple that blushed crimson, then orange. Several thin clouds of pure gold trailed above the brilliant orb. The cool air of sunset lifted Cassie's night-hued hair and kissed roses into her cheeks.

"I've enjoyed it here with you," she said contentedly. "This has been the best vacation I've ever had."

"Mine, too. But I have a feeling I would say the same thing no matter where we went. I love you, Cassie. Just being with you is a pleasure. The place doesn't matter."

She watched a purple wave rear up, roll toward the

beach and crash over in tumbling silver spray. At once it flattened and glided like quicksilver over the smooth sand. "I feel the same way about you, Luke. I'm so glad you came with me." She pressed her palm to his, enjoying the warm hardness of his hand.

"What would you like to do tomorrow?" he asked. "We've driven to Rand and seen the ghost town; we've seen miles of desert. We toured the movie lots and walked all over Los Angeles. What next? You know, we never did get to that restaurant the travel agent recommended."

Since their arrival in California, Cassie had decided that the idea of testing Luke was ludicrous and had done her best to rid her mind of the doubts caused by Trina's dire warning. However, she had not been completely successful. From time to time the ugly, black thoughts tried to wedge themselves between her and Luke, and when they did, she moved quickly to change things. Luke's mention of the restaurant had triggered them again. This time a change in location seemed called for.

Cassie smiled up at him. "You're right. I completely forgot about it. But you know what I'd really like to do? I'd like to leave tomorrow and fly to Denver."

"Colorado? What for?"

"To see the mountains, of course. Since we have to fly over them to get home, we may as well stop in Denver for a day or two."

"You're the most spontaneous person I ever met. Didn't anyone ever tell you that you're supposed to plan out a vacation and follow a schedule?"

"Why?"

"Because that's the way it's done. You don't go to the seashore *and* the mountains in the same trip."

"Why not?"

Luke thought for a minute. "I don't know."

"It's not like we have to go out of our way to get there. You could think of it as a pit stop."

"All right. I'll call and make arrangements when we get back to the bungalow. Do you want to stay anywhere in particular?"

"Let's decide when we get there." She shivered in anticipation. "There's so much I want to see and do!" Cassie continued. "I've never traveled very much, and now I can. I want to see London and Paris and Switzerland and all those other places you see on travel posters. Maybe I'll go to night school and learn to speak a foreign language—maybe two languages! Wouldn't you love to see a sunrise on the Sahara or a sunset in the Alps or a thunderstorm in Rome? I've heard they have tremendous storms there."

"Not this trip. I have a job, remember? Monday morning I have to be back at work." He smiled, but his voice was noticeably tight.

"I don't mean we should go there now," Cassie said. "I only meant I want to see those places someday." She matched her steps to his and gazed thoughtfully at the darkening sky. When she had had little money, it had been easy to say she wanted to spend all her time traveling, yet now that she could afford to do just that, she really wasn't so sure. In fact, she had begun to miss having a job and a regular schedule. All this freedom was a bit frightening at times.

"I'm looking forward to Colorado," she said after a while to reinforce her decision. After a moment's thought she added, "And I think I'll take a course to conquer my fear of flying."

She didn't notice how quiet Luke had become.

They drove toward the snow-cloaked mountains and soon left Denver behind. A light powder of new snow blanketed the fields and slopes, and ice creaked in the bare trees. Cassie snuggled her chin into the deep cowl of her warm cotton sweater and was glad she had brought some heavy clothes "just in case."

Before long the foothills became small mountains, and as their car emerged from a canyon drive, Cassie and Luke suddenly found they were in the midst of the majestic Rockies. Snowy peaks piled in tumbled profusion as far as they could see. The road was clear, but the leaden sky promised more flurries were on the way.

They drove until they reached Estes Park, nestled in its broad valley. Too late for summer vacationers and too early for skiers, the small town was relatively quiet. Just beyond the city they found a cluster of cabins on a sloping hillside and rented one near a rushing stream.

"Which do you like best?" Cassie asked as they climbed the front steps. "The beach or the mountains?"

Luke looked around at the impressive panorama. "First I liked the beach best, but having come here, I think I like this best. What about you?"

"I can't decide either. One thing is for sure, though

—I'm not swimming in *this* water." She nodded toward the clots of ice that tangled in last summer's grass by the stream.

"Neither am I. Come on in and let's get a fire started."

Without removing his coat, Luke knelt and arranged the kindling and logs for a fire. By the time he got it started, Cassie had found the thermostat and heat was beginning to take the chill from the room. She sat on the tweed couch and propped her feet up on the coffee table as she drank in the view from the expansive picture window.

Luke leaned the sooty poker against the log wall and came to sit beside her. After a while he said, "We seem to be in another world. No ocean, no gingerbread houses like we see in Plymouth. None of the Spanish style of California."

"Yet by air it's only a matter of hours to my home." She leaned back against him, and Luke circled her with his arms. "Maybe we could come back when the ski trails are open. Do you ski?"

"I used to." He didn't like to hear her talk about so much travel. Going on a vacation with her once at her expense was one thing, but he had no intention of making a habit of it. There was no way he could be comfortable if she was always paying his way.

"I've never tried. Trina and Dick ski in Vermont nearly every winter, but I've never been. Will you teach me how?"

"Sure, if you want me to. We can ski a lot closer to home, though. Let's drive up for a weekend when the trails open." Luke earned a comfortable income, but his salary couldn't stretch to include several trips to Colorado this winter.

"All right. Tell me what I'll need and I'll get it."

"We can rent it," he said abruptly. She seemed to think nothing of buying all that expensive equipment, he mused. Was all that money changing her? He had to smile—he hadn't known her before her windfall. Not really. Still, she hadn't impressed him as being a spendthrift.

"Look," Cassie exclaimed, "it's snowing!"

Soft flakes were drifting past the window. In moments a shimmering fog of white obscured the view. Cassie stood and put her coat back on. "We'd better bring in the luggage and the sack of groceries before it gets any worse."

Luke unwound his long frame and shrugged into his own coat. "It looks as if it could snow all night, from the way it's coming down."

"What if we get snowed in?" Cassie teased as she pulled her red knit cap over her ears. "Maybe you won't get back by Monday after all and we'll have to stay up here and play in the snow for days."

"If it gets that deep, the snowplow will be by when it lets up." He was zipping his coat and hadn't noticed she was joking. "I also saw a small plow down at the main lodge. We won't have to worry about getting stranded."

"Good," she said, feeling rebuffed. He sounded as if he didn't want to be snowbound with her.

They went back to the car and loaded themselves up to carry everything in one trip. Cassie squinted against the stinging flakes and tried to make out the mountains. Already the snow was obliterating the view and was blanketing the tracks they had made in the old snow.

"Why is it that snow is so pretty when it's not on your own doorstep?" she wondered aloud as she carried her load inside and set it on the floor.

"I guess because you don't have to shovel it. I like snow, but after a couple of months of it, I remember North Carolina with a great deal of longing."

"You didn't have snow there?"

"Not like in Plymouth, and it melted pretty fast."

"Now when I'm digging down to my front walk, all I'll be thinking of is North Carolina."

Luke took her in his arms and kissed her tenderly. "I'll make the supreme sacrifice and shovel your walk for you."

"We'll compromise and both of us will shovel it." Cassie laughed, then grew more serious. "Will you still be around when the walk needs shoveling?"

"I hope so," he replied softly. He could only hope she would still be content with an engineer who made less in one year than her new car had cost.

Cassie forced a smile to her lips and quickly looked away to the fire. She had expected him to say he wanted always to be with her. "You keep the fire going while I start supper. I sure hope this cabin is as well stocked with pans and utensils as the man at the desk promised."

As she clattered around in the tiny kitchen, Luke carried their luggage into the adjoining bedroom.

"This is great!" he called back to her. "There are windows on all three sides. We can open the curtains and pretend we're sleeping outside. Hey! I see a little pond down there. I wonder if it's frozen solid enough to skate on."

"Maybe." As she unpacked the steaks, potatoes and salad ingredients, she pondered over the man in the next room. He seemed to be having as much fun as she was, but occasionally she sensed a withdrawing. And he hadn't told her he wanted to be with her on a long-term basis. If he loved her, why didn't he?

Cassie closed her eyes, gripped the head of lettuce and called out, "Luke, would you like to move in with me?" She waited, all her muscles tensed at her daring.

The cabin was very quiet. Finally Luke said, "Maybe that's not a good idea just yet." He laughed, but the sound had a strained quality. "I don't want people to say I'm after your money."

"No," she answered with brittle cheerfulness, "we certainly wouldn't want that." She grabbed a bowl and started tearing the lettuce to shreds. There it was again. That damned money!

Luke came back to the door of the bedroom and leaned his forearm against the jamb. The light from the windows silhouetted his lean figure but his face was partially shadowed. "I'm very flattered you asked me," he said gently. "Do you understand why I can't?"

"What?" Cassie asked with feigned indifference. "Oh, sure. Don't give it another thought. Hey, the fire's burning low. Will you add another log?" She bent and buried her head in the cabinet, ostensibly in search of a skillet but actually to hide her tears.

Trina was right! Luke didn't want to live with her. He only wanted her money! How could she have been so mistaken? she berated herself. True, she wasn't very experienced with men, but even a child should have seen what was going on. The threatening tears spilled over and she shoved them angrily from her cheeks.

What was she going to do? Logic told her she should just bail out, but she still loved him. She wiped her eyes on a cup towel, still crouching behind the cabinets. She was caught in a triangle she had never expected: she loved a man; he loved her money. The three of them could have been very happy together. But not now that she knew.

"What are you doing back there?" Luke asked as he came into the kitchen.

"I'm looking for a skillet to cook the steaks," she said in a muffled voice.

"Let's broil them. There's a double oven. We can bake the potatoes at the same time.

"Okay. Wash the potatoes." Cassie pretended to be moving the pans back into place as she wiped away the last of her tears. Whatever other mistake she made, she wasn't about to let him see her cry.

Luke whistled a tune as he took the two potatoes from the sack and shoved up his sleeves. Cassie couldn't keep her heart from yearning for him as she watched him perform the domestic chore. His broad shoulders stretched the cotton weave of his cream-colored sweater. His jeans curved tightly over his firmly rounded buttocks and around his muscled thighs. As he scrubbed the potatoes, she saw the tendons flex in his forearms where sun-bleached hair was sprinkled over his tanned skin.

"How's that?" he asked. "Does that look clean enough to you?"

"That's fine," she answered, turning back to the salad. They couldn't possibly eat this much salad, but she was letting out her frustration by tearing the lettuce to bits.

"Next summer, would you like to go to the Cape? We can go in late May or early June and miss some of the tourists."

"Sure." Her voice was the one to sound tight now. Everyone knew how expensive the Cape was. Rooms were hard to find and cost far more than she had ever dared pay before. Luke certainly didn't seem reluctant to spend her money. To cover her agitation, she cleared her throat. "Will you have vacation time then?"

"I get two weeks, twice a year." He thought of Skip and Kelley's summer place. They had loaned it to him before and he was pretty sure they would let him use it again. All they would have to take were food and clothing. He was about to describe it to Cassie but changed his mind. He wanted to surprise her the way she had surprised him with this vacation.

Cassie turned on the oven and banged the broiler pan down on the cabinet. She desperately wished Trina had been wrong, but clearly she was right. If only someone else had discovered Luke was after nothing more than a good time! Knowing Trina, Cassie would hear about it for the rest of her life.

She glanced over her shoulder to see Luke searching in the cabinet for aluminum foil. Cassie pulled the box from the drawer beside her and pushed it within his reach. He grinned at her and her heart flipped.

Now that she knew, why was she still so attracted to him? Surely he shouldn't still seem so killingly handsome, so sexy. Light from the window turned his hair to dark flame, and his eyes were as clear as the green of springtime.

"What are you thinking?" he asked curiously.

"I was wondering if there's any dish soap for later."

"Under the sink. This place has everything. We should come back here again."

"Yes. We should." Cassie took a large knife and hacked the tomato into bits.

When the meal was cooked, they ate by the fire. Snow still fell outside, and under different circumstances Cassie would have felt satisfied and cozy in such a romantic setting. But all she could think of was how much Luke seemed to be enjoying himself. The fact that she had intended for him to do just that had slipped from her mind. When he offered to do the dishes, she put up only a token resistance, then gave in.

She sat staring into the fire, toasting on one side and seeming to freeze by contrast on the other. As she saw the situation, she had two options. She could never see Luke again, in which case her heart would break and she would be miserable, or she could continue on as if Trina had said nothing at all. She cast a furtive glance toward the open kitchen where Luke was putting the last pan into the dishwasher. She still loved him—that was the bad part. Otherwise she could turn her back on him and chalk this whole affair up as an unpleasant mistake. But she still wanted to touch him and kiss him and hear his voice.

Turning back to the fire, she rested her chin on her updrawn knees. Perhaps there was a third alternative. If she could make Luke truly fall in love with her, all her troubles would be over. A hint of a smile tilted her lips as she studied the flames through narrowed lids. She was no paragon of beauty, but neither was she all that unattractive. He already seemed to like her—nobody was that good an actor—and from that basis love might grow.

She sensed him nearing her and her pulse quickened. As he lowered himself down beside her on the thick rug, she said in a sweet tone, "Thank you for doing the dishes."

He glanced at her oddly. "You don't have to thank me. I ate half the meal."

"Just the same, I appreciate it." She looked over at him, tilting her head so that the firelight played across her cheekbones, and she lowered her lashes coquettishly. She had seen this done in movies.

"Are you feeling all right?"

"Marvelous!" She stretched sensuously, pulling her sweater snugly across her breasts and arching her back lithely. "I feel wonderful!"

"Good." He studied her for a bit, then leaned toward the grate to add another log.

Cassie leaned toward him, her lips parted and moist. "It's still snowing outside."

"Yeah, it's really coming down."

"I feel so snug in here," she breathed. "So safe."

"Are you sure you feel all right?" he asked again.

"Perfectly," she purred.

Luke straightened and propped his forearm on one bent knee. She was acting strange all of a sudden, but with Cassie he was beginning to consider mercurial changes to be normal.

Suddenly she threw herself against him and he tumbled over with her on top of him. He opened his mouth to ask why she had tackled him, but Cassie covered his lips with her own, cutting off his words.

Her warm tongue smoothed over his lips and explored the inner recesses of his mouth. Luke put his arms around her and held her to his chest, then ran his hand over the pleasing curve of her jean-clad derrière. She responded by moving rhythmically against him, and he slipped his fingers beneath her waistband to caress her soft skin.

As always at his touch, Cassie felt an urgency build within her. Absently she recognized that she might not be inspiring love, but she had certainly aroused an emotion that resembled it. As she gave herself to his expert caresses, she wondered how a woman could teach a man to love her. Whatever it might take, she was willing to do it. She loved Luke enough for them both.

Luke tasted the sweetness of her fire-warmed skin and marveled at the amount of love he felt for this woman he had known so short a time. If his love for her kept increasing at this rate, he wouldn't be able to let her out of his sight by Christmas. The prospect was very pleasing. He didn't want to let her out of his sight now.

He rolled her over and ran his hands under her sweater, and he felt her move eagerly to him. More than anything he wanted to live with her, but not the way she had suggested. He wanted her to marry him. As he stroked her creamy flesh, he wondered if that would be possible. There was no doubt in his mind that Cassie loved him, but would everyone always assume he had married her for her money? Even though she would never believe it, such an accusation would hurt her, and he couldn't bear that. Surely he could find a way to solve this problem, but at the moment her breast was swelling sensuously against his hand and she was nibbling the sensitive spot beneath his ear.

Luke quit thinking and gave himself up to the joy of loving Cassie.

Cassie knelt beside the sweeping branches of the snow-laden fir and followed Luke's pointing finger. In the clearing beyond, three deer moved restlessly. Luke and Cassie remained still as the animals pawed at the snow to uncover the brown grass. The largest of the three lifted his antlered head nervously and scented the air. As if by common agreement, the two does moved behind him toward the trees. Still looking about for the sensed but unseen danger, the animals melted into the protective shadows of the woods.

Slowly Cassie stood and flexed her cramped legs.

"Weren't they beautiful? I've never been so close to a wild animal."

"This is the best kind of hunting," Luke agreed as they strolled beneath the towering trees. "I'm glad you're not the sort to insist on sleeping late."

"We didn't do much sleeping at all," she pointed out contentedly. "We're probably getting more rest out here walking in the woods than we would have by staying in bed."

"I think you're right," he agreed with a grin.

The sun had come out and the sky was achingly blue. Against its brilliance, the evergreens were so dark as to be almost black. Nothing marred the expanses of fresh snow.

"I'm glad we found this place together," Cassie said as she stooped under a low limb. "It's as if we're the only people who have ever been here. From this angle I can't see a cabin or a road. This is what it must have looked like to the first pioneer woman."

"Probably. Only, to a pioneer, the snow falling this early would bring worry about a hard winter."

"Not if she had a good man like you," Cassie continued the pretense. "Her smokehouse would be full and her larder overflowing." She caught herself and blushed self-consciously. That had sounded like a blatant hint, and Luke had already refused to move in with her. To cover her embarrassment, Cassie pulled her cap lower and shoved her gloved hands deeper into her pockets.

"Is that how you see me?" Luke asked.

He wasn't going to drop it. Her cheeks flamed

uncomfortably and she nodded without looking at him. "Yes, I do."

Luke smiled and put his arm around her. He had no idea why she was blushing, but he found it endearing. He liked to think he could have mastered the wilderness as well as any pioneer, and he especially liked that Cassie thought so.

"I guess this is our last full day here," he commented after a while. "We fly back tomorrow."

"Maybe the airport is closed?" she asked hopefully.

"No, I heard on the radio that everything is open. We won't have any trouble taking off." She was so nervous about flying, he wanted to put her at ease.

"That's nice," she said with no conviction at all.

The snow crunched beneath their feet, and the only other sound was the occasional plop of an overloaded limb dropping its burden of snow. Cassie linked her arm around his waist and he hugged her close. Somehow when they were out playing in the wilds or on a deserted beach, the problem of her money seemed nonexistent.

Most of the night had been spent in Luke's arms, but there had also been ample time to think. Just before dawn Cassie had reached a conclusion. She loved Luke with every atom of her body, and she would be a fool to end her happiness. If Luke was only after her money, she had enough to keep him happy. It wasn't the way she wanted it, but things could be a lot worse. She was going to enjoy his attentions for as long as she could.

"You know," Luke said, completely oblivious to her train of thought, "this is when we're happiest. I enjoyed those fine restaurants in Los Angeles and the expensive hotel, but I like the log cabin even more. Now think about it. Weren't you happier out on the beach and here in the woods than you were in those places that cost a lot of money?"

"Yes," she said with surprise. "I've enjoyed walking in the snow and seeing those deer. And I'll always remember skinny-dipping with our clothes on and nearly freezing, and walking on the beach with sunset all around us. Those were special times."

"Good," Luke said with deep satisfaction. "Good."

Cassie didn't understand his sigh of relief, nor did she ask. She was content simply to walk beside him in the snow. All too soon they would be gobbled up again by civilization, and she didn't want to tarnish this last day by asking questions when she might hear an answer she wouldn't like.

When their feet grew too cold for comfort, they went back to the small cabin and spent the remainder of the day lying in each other's arms in front of the fire. Cassie couldn't recall ever having been happier. She refused to think about their pending departure; when she did, it seemed a dire threat to her newly found happiness. Luke, too, was uncommonly quiet, and Cassie decided to pretend his silence meant he also hated to see their romantic interlude come to an end.

8

Going in the front door of the Daisy Dilly Flower Shoppe gave Cassie an odd feeling, rather like ringing her own doorbell. She was greeted by a girl who looked young enough to still be in high school. Her jaws were champing rhythmically on a wad of gum and her big blue eyes were not wells of intelligence.

"Hello," Cassie said, when the girl merely waited for her to speak. "Is Mr. Glass in?"

"Yeah, but he's busy unloading some plants, you know. Can I help you? I'm the manager."

"You are?" Cassie couldn't hide her surprise. "My name is Cassie Collins and I really need to speak with Mr. Glass. Could I go back?"

"Nope. I can't let anybody past these doors." The girl nodded toward the batwing doors.

"I'll wait." Cassie turned away to look at the

flowers. A mere glance told her they needed water. Helpfully she said, "The gloxinias seem a little dry."

"You mean those funny-looking purple flowers? I thought maybe they're supposed to look that way. Some flowers are really strange, you know."

Cassie touched the wilting leaves and stated firmly, "They definitely need water." The shelves were dusty, too, and the dieffenbachias needed turning, but she refrained from pointing it out.

The back door banged shut and Cassie heard the sound of her former boss washing his hands. To the girl she said, "He seems to be through unloading. Will you tell him I'm here?"

"Sure. Sandy Collins, you said?"

"*Cassie* Collins. He'll know who I am."

The girl swished away, her tennis shoes keeping perfect time with her chewing gum. Cassie shook her head and sighed. The girl was exactly the type to wear the ridiculous red slickered apron. She heard an exchange of voices, then Elwin's balding head peered over the batwing doors and then withdrew. His expression had not been welcoming, and Cassie wondered uneasily if she should have come at all.

After he had kept her waiting for several additional minutes, Elwin Glass brushed through the swinging doors as if he were making a royal appearance. "Hello, Cassie. Are you interested in buying flowers?"

"No, actually I'm here for another reason. I was wondering if I could have my job back."

"Gone through all that money so quickly?" Elwin questioned with a lemony smile. "What a pity."

Cassie controlled her rush of anger. "I haven't spent my money. I only want my job back."

"You want your job back," Elwin repeated. "Now let me see. You still don't need the money, I would still be bothered with your groupies dropping by during business hours, but you think I ought to hire you back. In a word—no." He turned to leave, but Cassie darted around in front of him.

"You can't tell me *she*," Cassie said as she jerked her head toward the back, "is doing as good a job as I did! Just look at these flowers!"

"Maribeth is still learning." He narrowed his eyes at Cassie. "I don't suppose you'd work simply for the enjoyment of working?"

"You mean without any salary at all? Of course not. You weren't paying me much to start with."

"I was paying you more than I pay Maribeth."

"I did a better job. Mr. Glass, these flowers are dying! And the entire showroom needs a thorough cleaning."

"Since you no longer work here, that's none of your business."

"So you won't hire me back?"

"Very perceptive of you. No."

Cassie glared at him. "I'll try your competitors," she warned.

"We do what we have to do," he said with studied boredom. "Have at it."

Cassie left quickly before she said something she would regret. Her threat that she would try the other florists was an idle one, for she had already done so. Daisy Dilly had been her last choice.

As she drove away, she again mulled over the idea she'd had of starting her own shop. At first it had seemed absurd to create a business of her own just so she would have a job, but now it looked like the only way, so she decided she would. She drove to a realtor's office before she had time to get cold feet, and was soon on her way to see some prospective locations.

The first four were out of the question. One was pretty but overpriced for the neighborhood. Two of the others were in good areas but were too dark for flowers to thrive. The fourth would have required as much money to repair the roof and foundation as the asking price.

The last place she was chauffeured to was in the group of restored houses where Cassie had originally wanted to buy. The house was on a corner lot with ample room for parking and would be easy for customers to find. The front porch was deep and wide and could be glassed in to make a lovely showroom. The main room in the house was bright with sunshine from large windows, and the kitchen was well situated for a workroom. As a home, the place would be hard to sell, but as a florist shop it was perfect.

"I'll take it," Cassie said. Already she was mentally banking ferns and geraniums beneath the windows.

"Fine. Let's go back to the office and see what we can work out in terms of financing," the realtor said. "We have several lending institutions we deal with, and considering how high interest rates are in general, we have a couple of very attractive deals, if you can qualify for the loan."

"I plan to pay cash."

"Cash?" The realtor apparently hadn't heard of Cassie and the lottery.

"Yes, it's much less costly in the long run." Cassie looked about, deciding to paint the walls a pale yellow and to replace the worn carpet with a no-wax flooring.

When all the arrangements were made at the realtor's office, Cassie drove back to the house and parked in the drive. She had a lot to do before she could open. The painting and flooring had to be done and she had to find someone to enclose the porch. Hastily she made notes on a pad. Someone would have to pave the parking lot. She would have to have a sign painted, and she'd have to decide what kind of advertising to do. And she would need at least one full-time employee and some part-time help.

Cassie tapped the pencil against her cheek. Sudden inspiration made her smile. Laura! She had worked at the Daisy Dilly for a few months the year before, so she had some experience. Besides that, Laura was trustworthy and honest. Cassie would have no qualms about making her the manager. Most important of all, she knew Laura needed the job. If her husband, Tom, was laid off, their money would dribble to a halt.

Cassie drove to Laura's house and wound her way through the usual clutter of skateboards and tricycles to reach the porch.

Mark opened the door and let Cassie in before he ran through the house shrieking for his mother's attention. Cassie pushed aside a doll and sat on the couch. She was so glad she had thought of Laura. She suspected that not only would the money be welcome, but Laura might be eager to have a job that would get her out of the house. She didn't seem to be very happy as a full-time wife and mother. And lastly, this might mend the rift in their friendship.

Laura came in with her youngest daughter, Kathy, clutching her leg. "Hi, Cassie. I didn't expect you today." Her attitude wasn't as friendly as Cassie had hoped. The details of the argument they had had the last time she was there came back into focus.

"I guess I should have called first. How's Kathy feeling?"

"She's gotten better. Now Tommy and Janie have it." Laura sat on the arm of an overstuffed chair and swung her leg in a nervous gesture.

This wasn't going as well as Cassie wished. "Laura, I have a great idea. I'm going to open my own flower shop."

Laura waited for her to continue.

Cassie bit her lower lip and continued, "Elwin Glass won't hire me back and I want to work. None of the other shops are hiring, so I thought I ought to start one of my own. What do you think?"

"I think it's great to be able to create your own job like that. It's a shame Tom can't. He's going to be out of work starting next week unless the union can finish negotiations."

Cassie took a deep breath. "I want you to manage the shop."

"Me? I have all I can do now." Laura gestured at the clean but cluttered room. "You know Kathy and Mark aren't in school yet, and Timothy takes so much of my time."

"Your salary would pay for day care."

"I don't know," Laura said reluctantly. "Putting the kids in day care doesn't seem like a very good idea. You hear so much about what goes on in those places."

"Those are the exceptions. Laura, I can pay you a good salary."

Laura gave her a long look as Kathy turned suddenly shy and tried to bury her face in her mother's stomach. In the background, Janie set up a whining cry, echoed by Mark who wanted a forbidden cookie.

"It would get you out of the house," Cassie pointed out.

"What makes you think I want out?" Laura asked huffily. "I love my kids." She fended Kathy off by handing her a plush toy.

"I know you do. That's not what I meant."

"You think we'll need the money, with Tom out of work."

"Well, who wouldn't? It's not a disgrace."

"Cassie, I told you we don't take charity." Laura's voice was strained with emotion.

"It's not charity! I need a manager for my store."

"I can tell you now that it won't be me! I have a family to raise and a husband to take care of. I can't go waltzing off to work in a flower shop."

"You make it sound as if I'm planning an outing on the Riviera!"

"I wouldn't know about the Riviera. *I'm* not a jet-setter."

"Neither am I! You know I don't go to places like that."

"So what's stopping you? You have plenty of money, no family to tie you down!" Her words were accusatory, as if Cassie had somehow failed by not having a family by this time.

Cassie tried to control herself. "I don't know why we're arguing again. All I did was offer you a job."

"You offered me charity." Laura lifted her head proudly, as Janie's wails increased in volume in the other room.

"I'll work your buns off!" Cassie offered. "Six days a week! No vacation! Does that make you happier?"

"I just guess you would like that! Then you could say you gave charity and got slave labor in exchange."

"How can you say that!" Cassie glared at her friend. "I don't know who you are anymore!"

"I guess with your college degree and all that money, we don't have anything in common." Laura's eyes misted with tears and her voice shook, but she maintained a rigid posture. "Maybe someday you'll get married and see what it's like to have a home to take care of."

"I have a home and you know it."

"Maybe you'll even have children someday," Laura continued. "And then you'll know why I won't leave them in some rotten day-care center . . ."

"So who told you to pick a rotten one?"

". . . to be mistreated or ignored or who knows what else."

"It's a job! A paying job!"

"I think you should leave now. My children need me." Laura drew motherhood about her like a protective cloak.

Cassie stared at her friend's tearstained cheeks. Slowly she stood. "Laura, you're a snob of the worst sort. If I had lost every penny I owned, you wouldn't turn your back on me. But because just the opposite happened, you don't want to be my friend. If that's how you want it, that's not all right, but I guess I'll have to learn to live with it." She turned away and went to the door. Without looking back, she added brokenly, "I won't be back unless you call me." As she left, she heard a muffled sob but she kept going. Her own misery was barely in check.

She had little memory of the ride home. Visions of Laura laughing with her in high school, of them making their grand plans to change the world, of double dates and all-night record sessions filled her mind. "I'm going to miss you, Laura," she whispered as she parked in her garage.

A cold wind was whipping off the water, and tall clouds sailed the horizon of the pewter sea. A storm was building offshore. Already the waves covered the beach and bit at the wall of granite rocks piled as a breakfront. Cassie hurried into the warmth of the house.

The telephone was ringing, and she lifted the kitchen extension. "Hello?" she answered breathlessly.

"Hello, Miss Collins? This is Jay Merriweather."

Cassie racked her brain to put a face to the familiar name. "I'm sorry, but I don't . . ."

"We met at a party. Luke Bennett works for me here at Pan-Ways."

"Oh, yes. I remember." Cassie's friendly tone

cooled as she also recalled the unpleasant scene Luke's boss had caused. "Why are you calling, Mr. Merriweather?"

"I have a little business proposition I thought you might be interested in. I have a lead on some commercial property that would be perfect for a strip center. You know, just a few stores, like a pharmacy and a convenience store. Maybe a couple of small business offices."

"Have you ever put together a successful business deal like this before?" Cassie suppressed her impatient sigh.

"No. Frankly, I've never had the financial backing." His laugh was hale and hearty, making her one of the team.

"What background do you have in arranging a real-estate deal?"

"Well, I know a contractor, and a lawyer who can handle all the legal details."

"Then why wouldn't I go out and contact a lawyer and a contractor for myself if I wanted to build a shopping center?"

"I'm willing to do all that for you. We'd be partners."

"I would supply the money? What would you contribute?"

"My time and my contacts. I've been around the block once or twice, so to speak, and I know the right people in the right places."

"I'm not interested," Cassie said, preparing to hang up. "Thank you for calling," she added when she remembered this was Luke's boss.

"But it's a hell of a deal! You don't seem to understand what you're passing up. Ask Bennett. He'll explain it to you. Hell, you'll get the money back inside a year!"

"Good-bye, Mr. Merriweather."

"Let me go over it again. I—"

"Mr. Merriweather, I hate to hang up on people," Cassie stated with exasperation. "It really spoils my day, and between you and me, I've already had a rotten day. Now you just say good-bye and let's end this gracefully."

"If you'd just listen—"

"Good-bye." Cassie hung up on Merriweather's irritated voice. Boss or no boss, she wasn't going to stay on the phone and be patronized, especially not when she suspected she was also being conned.

Cassie felt terrible. After the blowup with Laura and the unpleasantness with Merriweather, she felt physically ill. Conflict always had that effect on her. She went upstairs and took two aspirins, then started the shower.

After tossing her clothes into the hamper, she stepped under the stinging spray and let it sluice over her head. She lifted her hands to the soap and washcloth and scrubbed her body vigorously. At last her tension faded and she shampooed her hair, imagining the water rinsing away her troubles along with the soap.

She turned off the shower, and with a bath sheet wrapped around her, she blew her hair dry and put on makeup. She didn't know what time it was, but Luke would undoubtedly be there soon.

Feeling limp, she studied her reflection in the steamy mirror. She looked the same, felt the same, enjoyed the same things. So why was the money playing havoc with her entire life? Her reflection had no answer, so she hung her towel on the brass hook and went into her room to dress.

Trying not to give the matter further thought, she put on her lacy underwear and pulled on a lightweight wool dress in a cherry red that made her skin glow and her hair gleam like sable. As she stepped into her black lizard shoes, she heard the peal of the doorbell. A glance at the clock told her Luke was a little early. She was glad not to be alone with her thoughts any longer. She grabbed her heavy wool shawl and hurried downstairs.

Luke stood on her doorstep, wearing an English tweed sport coat in deep browns and slacks of dark umber. His shirt was cream and his tie was shades of brown and green. The strong wind rumpled his thick hair and brought a brightness to his green eyes.

Cassie felt a calm spread over her just from the sight of him. "You look so good," she breathed.

"So do you. I'm early."

"I'm glad you are. This has been one of those days." She wrapped her shawl about her and added, "I bought a flower shop—or what will be one—had a terrible argument with Laura and hung up on your boss. Are you ready to go eat? I'm starved."

"Why does talking with you always make me feel dizzy?" He pulled her door shut and checked to see that it locked. "Merriweather called you? What about?"

"Another investment scheme. A strip center this time. I hope I didn't cause you any trouble, but I tried to be nice and he wouldn't let me."

"Merriweather's like that. Subtlety is not part of his makeup. Why did you argue with Laura?" He opened the car door for her, and she waited to answer until he came around and slid behind the wheel.

"Oh, Luke, it was terrible! I went over to offer her a job as manager of my flower shop, but she took it all wrong and said I was trying to give her charity. And I know she needs the money! Tom is being laid off and they have five little children."

"Maybe she's jealous," Luke suggested gently. "You seem to have everything—freedom to do as you please, no one depending on you to feed and clothe them, and above all, the money. Who wouldn't be a little jealous of someone who becomes a millionaire overnight?"

"You don't feel that way, do you?"

"No, but I love you."

Cassie looked out at the tree-lined street. The wind was stripping the limbs of their bright foliage and whirling eddies of russet and gold across the lawns. She felt sad, as if a season were ending for her, too. She wasn't sure she would ever again be able to live normally or to trust that her relationships would be founded on who she was and not what she owned. She glanced sideways at Luke. She couldn't even be sure about the man she loved.

The storm was coming closer, and huge waves were churning the sea to froth. Their booming voices could be heard even in the closed car as Cassie and Luke drove down the ocean-flanked road. Where the sea wall thwarted the waves, they splashed and boiled angrily as if they longed to cover the road and reach the houses that lay beyond.

Luke pulled into a restaurant parking lot that backed onto the sea. Here the deep water tossed enormous waves against and over the restraining wall. The small building seemed to huddle down on the slick pavement as the waves actually broke over the portion of the roof closest to the sea.

Cassie stared at the gray water. "The waves are so big," she said. "Do you think it's safe to eat here?"

"If it wasn't, the place would be closed. The storm is still well out to sea. We'll be home before it fully breaks."

Cassie opened the car door and hurriedly crossed the wet lot to the restaurant. Luke had called her house "home" as if he felt it was his own, yet he had refused to move in with her. Cassie couldn't help but wonder why. She wanted more than anything for him to be the way he seemed and to have no ulterior motives, but she couldn't figure him out.

They ordered fish and baked potatoes from the nervous waitress, who was more interested in watching the hungry waves than her order pad. Cassie also noticed the woman spent no more time than was necessary at the back of the restaurant where the waves pounded the windows.

"Are you sure this is safe?" Cassie asked Luke as another assault from the sea poured buckets of water over the window beside their table.

"This is an old building. It must have withstood years of storms, even hurricanes."

"Do you suppose all those storms could have weakened it?"

"Would you like to leave, or move to a table away from the windows? I didn't realize the storm was making you this nervous."

"No, this is all right." She decided she was already so upset that the waves couldn't do any more harm to her nerves. Besides, Luke was an engineer and she supposed he knew all about structural stress and things like that. Also, it was pretty novel to eat underneath breaking waves.

"How is your space suit design coming along?" she asked as they ate.

"Fine. I think I've run across an idea to make the gloves more flexible. Next week Bob Crippen and Judy Resnik will be coming up to look over the design."

"The astronauts? Really?"

"Do you want to meet them? They'll be in town several days. Maybe we can meet them for dinner one evening."

"I'd love it! Just imagine talking with real astronauts!"

Luke looked at her, then glanced away. She was awfully excited about meeting Crippen and Resnik. Was she turning into a social climber? He had spent years working with astronauts and had long since forgotten his own initial awe. To him they were business acquaintances, nothing more. His former girlfriend, Maureen, had also been eager to rub elbows with the great or even the near-great. She had been an incurable name-dropper and had collected introductions like scalps. Was Cassie beginning to show the same unpleasant tendency?

"Tell me about your flower shop," he said to break his thoughts.

"It's perfect. You're going to love it!" She launched into a detailed description, skipping so erratically from room to room that Luke was left thoroughly confused. "I'm going to buy paint and start refinishing it as soon as I can close on it. What do you think about yellow? Nothing glaring, but soft to suggest sunshine?"

"Sounds good. But why not hire it done? You can certainly afford it."

"I know, but I like to paint. Besides, I have nothing to do all day. I need to be working."

Luke hardly heard her answer. His mind was running over earlier conversations with her, searching for signs of whether the money was affecting her. He dreaded seeing her change, but she seemed to be doing it.

When Luke didn't reply, Cassie pushed her plate aside and pretended to watch the waves, although now all she could see was a wet glass. Was he upset because she didn't want to hire the paint job done? What if they did get married and he expected her to sit around and do nothing all day! She wasn't the sort to hire every little chore done, even if she could afford it.

"I'm thinking of putting in a swimming pool for next summer," she said to cover the awkward silence. "How do you think one would be back toward the rose bed?"

"I think leaves from that big maple tree would fall in it. That's near the poplar, too. You'd have to clean it too often." He didn't know what pools cost, but he knew they weren't cheap. At her crestfallen look, he said, "But you could hire a maintenance man to clean it. Or you could even enclose it to keep leaves out and then you could use it all year around."

Cassie had never priced pool enclosures, but she suspected that could run to more expense than the modest pool she had in mind. "Maybe. I'll think about it."

Luke paid the waitress and helped Cassie wrap herself in her tartan shawl. "I like this. Is it new?"

She nodded absently. The dress and shawl had been on sale for a price she couldn't pass up. Cassie loved bargains.

Luke fingered the soft wool. He knew expensive clothes when he saw them. Keeping his tone light, he said, "It makes you look like an authentic Highlander."

Cassie managed to smile but the effort made her face feel as if it might crack. If they married, would he expect her to become a fashion plate? She enjoyed pretty clothes, but she was really more comfortable in jeans and an old sweat shirt.

They were both quiet on the drive back to Cassie's house. Night was falling fast and the sky went from a brassy gray to dull black without a blush. Thunder could be heard in the distance and the waves beat at the beach.

Luke followed Cassie inside and automatically bent

to pet Phuzzbott when the cat trotted out to meet him. "Somebody ought to tell Phuzzbott that cats aren't supposed to be affectionate," he said as the cat curled around his ankle.

"He failed aloofness in cat college. He was Aunt Cassandra's pet, and she raised him to think he's a dog. He even comes when you whistle or call his name." Cassie watched Luke stroke the animal. All her life she had maintained that an animal was a good barometer of a person's true character. If that was true, she mused, Luke must be all he seemed, because Phuzzbott always made a fool of himself to get Luke's attention.

Abruptly she said, "Will you spend the night with me?"

He stood up. "Of course. Is the storm making you nervous?"

"No. I just want to lie beside you all night." In his loving arms she knew she would be free of her doubts and fears.

He came to her and held her close. "I love you, Cassie."

"I love you, too."

As they walked arm in arm toward the stairs, Luke wondered if he would be able to say no if she asked him again to move in with her. Every day he loved her more, yet there was this facet of her that surfaced from time to time, her desire to become a jet-setting butterfly. That was not something he felt he could live with. He knew that he was basically very traditional. To him, a love relationship meant marriage, and for that the couple needed to be sure they were well matched. But then a small voice inside reminded him of the love he felt for Cassie in spite of their differences, and he cocked his head to one side in puzzlement.

As he passed the light switch at the head of the stairs, he automatically flipped it off, plunging the lower floor into darkness. As they headed toward the bedroom, Luke tried to leave his doubts behind.

9

As Cassie plugged in the percolator, she heard Luke whistling in the shower upstairs. Occasionally the whistle broke off in midnote and she pictured him reaching for the soap or rinsing his head under the water. He sounded particularly happy, and after the long night of loving, she was still floating on a cloud of euphoria. Never had she dreamed that she could experience so much love. The most wonderful part was that no matter how much she loved him, Luke accepted it with open arms and gave her back at least as much in return.

Feeling particularly domestic this morning, Cassie found her seldom-used recipe for biscuits and started searching for her measuring cup. More than anything she wanted to hear Luke upstairs every morning and know he would come home to her every night. She thought maybe a pan of homemade biscuits might help her achieve that end. Aunt Cassandra had often expounded that the way to a man's heart was through his stomach. Cassie knew there was more to it than that, but if there wasn't at least a grain of truth, why had the saying become an adage?

She measured out some flour and dumped it into a mixing bowl, sending a fine spray of white powder over her hands and the counter top. Disregarding the mess, she brushed her hair back, leaving a pale smudge on her cheek, ear and dark hair.

The phone rang and Cassie answered, balancing the receiver between her cheek and shoulder as she reached to turn on the oven. "Hello?" she sang out cheerfully.

"Good morning, Miss Collins. You sound chipper today." The man's voice was unpleasantly familiar.

"Mr. Merriweather?" she asked uncertainly.

"That's right. Have you considered the investment I spoke to you about? I know I haven't given you much time to mull it over, but we need to step in before someone beats us to it."

"I don't believe this!" Cassie exclaimed, some of her good mood evaporating.

"I just got off the phone with the man who owns the land. He's an old army buddy of mine, and he's willing to give us until noon to make an offer before he opens bidding."

"Noon!"

"I couldn't very well ask a buddy to hold off indefinitely. It's not like he was a stranger. What do you say?"

"The same thing I said before. No! I can't believe you called me again on this. What does it take to get through to you?"

There was a pause, as if Merriweather was struggling to hold his temper. Then the jovial voice was back. "Have you talked to Bennett about this? I really think you should."

"Luke? What does he have to do with this?"

"We discussed it at work yesterday. That's one reason I called you instead of someone else. Bennett think's it's a grand idea."

"He does?" More of Cassie's good mood dissolved. The idea of Luke and his boss discussing ways to spend her money was very distressing.

"I was telling him what a good idea this strip center is, and he agreed it would make the owners a bundle of money and be an excellent tax shelter. And you need all the shelter you can get."

Cassie numbly reached for the baking soda and measured the correct amount into the bowl of flour. Her mind refused to imagine Luke doing this to her.

Merriweather took her silence for capitulation and continued, "Let's set a time for you to come look at the land. It's in a prime location, so we can't go wrong. Of course, you have to pay more for prime property like this, but it means more profit in the long run. What's a good time for you this morning?"

"No! Absolutely not! And if you call me again I'm going to report you to the phone company for harassing me." She slammed down the receiver so hard the bell jingled on the phone.

Angrily, Cassie measured out more baking soda

from the box and tossed it into the bowl, forgetting that she'd already done so. Her thoughts were seething at Merriweather's gall. She couldn't believe Luke would really try to pressure her into a deal, but why would Merriweather tell a lie that could so easily be proven false? Merriweather had encouraged her to ask Luke's advice in the phone call before, as well. What was going on?

Upstairs she heard Luke's whistle travel from the bathroom to the bedroom. She was going to ask him and get the matter straight, once and for all; but before she could leave the kitchen, she heard a rapping at the back door and turned to see Trina and her mother peering through the glass. With a nervous glance toward the ceiling, Cassie thrust her hair behind her ear and tightened the sash of her dark green velour robe. Maybe with luck she could get rid of them before Luke came downstairs.

She opened the door, and before she could speak her nephew darted in and ran toward the fishbowl in the living room, greeting her perfunctorily in passing. "Hello, Mom, Trina," Cassie said as the two women edged in and crossed the porch to the kitchen. "I'd like to visit, but—"

"It's freezing out there!" Trina interrupted. "Terry! You put that fishbowl down." To Cassie, she said, "Honestly, you'd think Dick could baby-sit sometime, wouldn't you? But no, he's off to play golf in this arctic air."

"Trina, you're exaggerating. It's not *that* cold," her mother corrected. "Terry, dear, we don't spin the fishbowl, do we?"

Cassie leaned around the corner and her eyes met her nephew's. "You may look at Mr. Beebles, but don't touch," she instructed.

Instantly the boy smiled obediently and quit whirling the bowl on the waxed coffee table. "Okay, Aunt Cassie."

Trina shook her head despondently. "I don't know how you do it, Cassie. Every time I tell Terry anything, it goes in one ear and comes out the other."

"We have an understanding. He minds me and I won't swat him," Cassie answered. To her mother she said, "Why are you out today?"

"There's a big sale at Bergman's. You've simply got to come with us."

"You're kidding, aren't you?" Trina asked, looking anxiously at Cassie. "You haven't really spanked him, have you? You know how I feel about that."

"Mom, this really isn't a good day for me to go shopping."

Cassie tried to judge how long it would take Luke to dress and come downstairs. "Maybe I could go Monday."

"The sale will be over then. We came all the way over here to get you."

"Cassie, you didn't *really* spank Terry, did you?" Trina repeated.

Cassie added another full measure of baking soda to the flour. "Mom, I really don't want to go. I'm sorry you drove all the way over here, but as you can see, I'm not dressed and . . ." Her sentence died in her throat as she heard Luke's light tread on the stairs.

Two seconds later Terry came running, round-eyed,

to the kitchen. "Mommy! There's a man coming downstairs!"

Cassie closed her eyes for a moment and tried hard to vanish.

"Good heavens!" her mother confirmed. "It *is* a man."

"Cassie!" Trina gasped in accusation.

Luke paused in the act of buttoning his shirt when he saw the group staring at him through the doorway. Then he recovered and finished buttoning his shirt as he went toward them. "Good morning," he said.

"Cassie!" Trina repeated, and glared at her sister.

"Mom, Trina, you remember Luke Bennett," Cassie said, trying to work her way out of the awkward situation with a show of manners.

"Who is he?" Terry demanded of his mother.

"My name is Luke," he said, squatting down to the boy's level. "I'll bet your name is Terry."

"That's right," the boy piped. "How did you know that?"

"Mr. Beebles told me," Luke answered with a broad grin.

Trina pulled her son to her and pressed his tow head against her skirt as if to protect him from an obvious danger. "Good morning, Mr. Bennett," she said icily.

"Coffee, anyone?" Cassie ventured.

Her mother swiveled her head around and gave Cassie a maternal look meant to wither an erring youth. "You might have told us you had company." Her voice was as cold as Trina's had been.

"Mom, I'm all grown up now," Cassie replied.

Her mother shot her a look that spoke volumes. "We had better go, Trina."

"Yes. I think we had."

"Mommy, did Aunt Cassie have a slumber party?" Terry asked as he was whisked away.

"Go get in the car, Terry," Trina ordered.

"Can I have a slumber party, too, Mommy?" Terry pursued as he was bundled out the door. "Can I invite all my friends and have ice cream?"

"Get in the car, Terry!" Trina's voice was muffled as the back door slammed behind her and her son.

"Mom," Cassie began, "it's not the way it must look. Luke and I love each other." Her dark eyes begged her mother to understand. "I'm not a child. I'm all grown up."

"You'll always be a child to me," her mother said stiffly. She passed a cursory look over Luke and fixed Cassie with her unyielding glare. "I just hope this hasn't marked Terry." She turned on her heel and marched out the back door.

"Mom, you're making too much of this," Cassie protested, but the slamming door obscured the last of her sentence.

Cassie raised her hands in a frustrated gesture, then let them drop back to her side. "I was afraid they would be upset."

"Honey, you *are* a grown woman," Luke reminded her as she came back into the kitchen.

"Not to them, I'm not. You saw their faces. Goodness knows what they'll tell Terry."

"They won't tell him anything. This will all blow over. Don't worry about it."

"You don't understand. I'm the baby of the family. They don't want to admit I'm grown up." She leaned against the counter.

"I guess it's a good thing I didn't move in with you," Luke mused as he put his arm around her.

"That's different. Don't you see? If you were living here, that would mean we've made a commitment to each other. This way it must look like . . . touch and go."

"That's not how you see us, is it?" Luke asked, lifting her chin with his forefinger.

"No. In a way. Oh, I don't know anymore!" Cassie's eyes were troubled and filled with hurt.

"Cassie, you know better than that. I love you, honey." He stroked the smudge of flour from her cheek. While he was showering he had thought long and hard about their relationship, and he had decided that his first decision had been correct. They were meant to be together. As he was coming downstairs, he had been deciding how and when to ask her to marry him. This seemed to be the best possible time.

"Don't turn away, honey. There's something I want to ask you." He pulled her back gently.

"Well, there's something I want to ask you, too." She put her hands against his chest and leaned back to study his expression. "Did you talk to Mr. Merriweather about an investment in a strip center?"

This was so far from what he had expected that Luke was caught off guard. "Yes, I think I remember his mentioning something like that." He racked his brain to recall. The conversation had happened yesterday. He and a group of co-workers had been taking a coffee break when Merriweather joined them. The discussion had swung from football to investments, and Merriweather had casually talked about his interest in buying a lot downtown to build a small shopping center.

"You did talk with him about it!" Cassie exclaimed. "And you told him that you thought what he was suggesting was a good idea?"

"Yes, I did." So had everyone else around the coffee machine. "So what?"

"So what?" Cassie shrugged out of his embrace and glared at him. "You're asking me so what?"

"Honey, did I miss something?" Luke asked in confusion.

"Don't you call me honey! In fact, don't call me at all! I'm not speaking to you."

"Will you tell me why?" Luke's voice was rising to match hers. "Calm down and let's talk about it."

"Don't you tell me to calm down! I'm perfectly calm, all things considered," she said as she thrust her fingers through her hair and then jabbed one at him accusingly. "And I'm not about to talk to you about this! You'd really like that, wouldn't you! So would Merriweather. You two think I'll eat out of your hand! Well, you have another think coming."

"What in the hell are you talking about!" Luke roared.

"That's right! Yell at me! I don't care," she yelled back.

"Why are we having a fight?" He glared at her angrily.

"Naturally, you'd be happier if I just gave in,

wouldn't you? Men!" The last word was spat out with vengeance. "Well, I'm not going to talk about it!"

"*What* aren't you going to talk about, damn it!"

"I think you had better leave," she stormed.

"Cassie, this is crazy!"

"Get out of here before I lose my temper!"

"You've already lost it!"

"Go away!" She turned her back to him and made a show of indifference as she added more baking soda to the bowl of flour.

Luke glared at her, but she refused to turn around. After a long moment he pivoted on his heel and stalked through the house, yanking his coat from the hall tree as he passed. He demonstrated his fury by slamming the front door behind him.

A cold wind cut at his face as he jerked on his coat and got in his car. He fished the keys out of his pocket as he sat glaring at the house.

She was nuts, he decided as he spun out of the drive. Certifiably wacky! All night she had cuddled in his arms and loved him as completely as one person could love another; then she had blown up like that and he had no idea why.

Luke took a curve faster than was prudent and his wheels squealed in protest. He whacked the dashboard with the heel of his hand.

What had happened? he demanded. When they woke up she had been cuddly and sweet as only Cassie could be. Then he had taken a shower while she went downstairs. Nothing there to upset her—cooking had been her idea.

Disregarding the posted speed limit, Luke sped down the tree-domed streets, leaves whipping into a tempest in his wake.

Had he realized her family was there, he might have stayed upstairs until they were gone. Then again, he might not have. Never having faced that situation, Luke couldn't honestly say at this point what he would have done. At any rate, he wouldn't have come downstairs buttoning his shirt. He hadn't intended to embarrass Cassie in front of her family.

Was that it? She was remarkably shy about some things, and the reactions of her mother and Trina had been outraged shock. But damn it, Cassie was no sixteen-year-old virgin! She was a grown woman and responsible for making her own decisions about this sort of thing. It wasn't as if this were an overnight fling. They loved each other! He had been about to propose!

Luke turned into his parking lot and stalked to his apartment. He had no doubt that the embarrassment had upset her, but something else was disturbing her. He tried to figure out what it might be. Something about strip centers and Merriweather, Luke recalled. He let himself in and shut the door with a bang. What could Merriweather and shopping centers have to do with anything?

He went into the kitchen, filled a coffee cup with water and shoved it in the microwave. Merriweather. Shopping center. Surely it couldn't be.

The bell dinged to signal the water was hot. Luke poured in a spoonful of instant coffee and went back to the living room. Now that he thought about it, he had heard Cassie's phone ring while he was in the shower.

He frowned at the phone on his end table, then pulled the directory out of the magazine rack. He found the number he wanted and dialed. When a man answered, he said, "Mr. Merriweather, this is Luke Bennett. I was thinking about that idea you mentioned about the strip center. Have you said anything to Cassie Collins about that?"

He leaned back and listened as Merriweather told him about his conversation with Cassie. Luke's eyes narrowed to dangerous slits of jade, and his knuckles ridged white as he gripped the phone. "I see," he said when his boss had finished. "Well, I guess I have only one thing to say about that. If you call Cassie again for any reason, or ever imply to anyone else that I support your harebrained schemes, I'm going to break off your arm and stuff it in your ear." His tone was coolly pleasant, as if he were merely imparting a fact.

"No," Luke broke in on his boss's enraged retort, "this isn't a case of insubordination because I quit. You can take my job and shove it in your other ear."

He was almost enjoying this. "Monday you'll find my formal letter of resignation on your desk. I won't be there because I'm taking the other two weeks' vacation time you owe me."

Luke smiled at the pleasure he was deriving from all this. He had been on the verge of quitting for months. "No, Mr. Merriweather, I think your suggestion is anatomically impossible."

He dropped the receiver back onto the cradle,

silencing Merriweather's tirade. Slouching low in the chair, Luke sipped his coffee. That had felt good, he thought with satisfaction. What a pity he hadn't done it weeks ago and saved Cassie the hassle.

He started to dial her number but paused. She was pretty angry. Letting her have time to cool off might be a smarter move. Instead, he dialed the operator and asked for a number near Hartford. The International Fabrics Corporation was building a new facility in Plymouth, and their personnel director, whom Luke had known since college, had already contacted him to offer him a job with their space suit development group. Luke smiled as he waited for his friend to answer the phone. He had wanted to work for IFC from the beginning, but hadn't wanted to live in Connecticut. With the new location he wouldn't have to move.

The man answered and Luke's grin broadened. He should have done this months before.

Cassie stood glaring at the front door. She had told him to leave but she hadn't expected him to really do it. How could she have an argument with him if he wouldn't stay and fight?

She dumped the mixture of flour and baking soda in the wastebasket and rinsed the bowl. He really had some nerve, leaving in the middle of an argument. If she were speaking to him, she would call and tell him so. She unplugged the coffee pot and poured the contents down the sink.

Trina also had a nerve, Cassie fumed. She knew for a fact that her sister's white wedding gown had been a mere formality. Her shocked reaction when Luke walked into the kitchen was pure hypocrisy. It was clear from Terry's response that he had found nothing disturbing about it. Cassie tried not to even think about her mother's reaction.

Cassie went upstairs and dressed hurriedly. She had to get out and run on the beach or do something to get this adrenaline out of her system. On the spur of the moment, she punched out Luke's phone number. A busy signal buzzed in her ear. He certainly wasn't moping around, she thought angrily. No doubt he and his buddy Merriweather were cooking up their next get-rich-quick scheme.

The idea made stinging tears blur her eyes. She slammed the phone down and went to her closet. The beach wasn't far enough. She needed real distance to work out this much anger.

Shoving the tears off her cheeks, Cassie threw some clothing into her suitcase. She would go away for a few days. Get space between herself and her troubles. Maybe do a little early Christmas shopping.

Cassie hauled her suitcase out to the car. She never heard the phone ringing as she backed out of the drive.

10

Cassie wandered down the narrow streets of Salem, Massachusetts, and reflected how the old town's dark history mirrored her mood. She wasn't all that concerned about her mother and Trina's knowing that she and Luke were lovers. The way they had found out was embarrassing, but Cassie was entitled to make her own decisions. However, she was disconsolate after learning that Luke had been conspiring with his boss over ways to spend her money. And Luke had assured her that her money wasn't important to him!

She bought a ticket for a tour of the Witches' House and joined a small group that had already gathered inside. Cassie tried to concentrate as the guide, who was dressed in seventeenth-century costume, pointed out the warming pans and cooking utensils, but having grown up around such antiquities, the items held little interest. She followed the others up the narrow stairs for a view of the bedroom where, as the guide fervently pointed out, the hapless prisoners spent their last fearful hours before being tried and convicted of practicing witchcraft. The room looked pretty much like any bedroom of the period and, in fact, seemed less gloomy to Cassie than the family's common room downstairs. Had her mood been lighter, Cassie would surely have allowed her vivid imagination to sweep her back several centuries along with the other tourists, who were commenting to one another about how terrifying it must have been back then.

Remembering that this trip was supposed to be taking her mind off her troubles, Cassie made an effort to become interested in the ancient documents and records fixed on the walls. She realized belatedly that she should have chosen a more cheerful place to visit.

If only Trina had been wrong about Luke. She would give anything to have him love her the way he claimed he did. Obviously that was asking too much. How, she wondered, had she ever convinced herself that a man as handsome and intelligent as Luke could fall in love with a very average person like her? Cassie couldn't let the thought go.

As she left, she slipped a generous donation in the box set aside for funds to perpetuate the old town.

Outside, she looked up at the hazy white sky. Not cloudy enough to portend rain, but there would be no cheerful blue that day. Despondent, she returned to her room at the Hawthorne Hotel, sat on the end of her bed and flopped backward, arms outstretched, her fingers dangling down toward the floor. She had to do something. She couldn't wallow in self-pity for the rest of her life.

"Take charge," she instructed herself halfheartedly as she stared up at the stippled ceiling. "It's your life—control it."

The words were right, but without conviction they were merely platitudes. She only wanted one outcome, and that was to have Luke love her for herself alone.

For a few moments she toyed with the idea of visiting the shop of Laura Cabot, Salem's resident witch, to buy a love potion. She spun an unlikely fantasy in which she mixed an exotic powder into Luke's coffee and, with a pink puff of smoke, Luke became her wholehearted lover. With a sigh, Cassie sat up. There was no magic potion. Even if there were, she wouldn't use it. She wanted Luke to come to her on his own, but that was clearly impossible. The money wasn't going to go away, and Luke had lied to her about his interest in her money. She blinked back a tear that threatened to brim over.

Nothing would be gained by sitting around, falling deeper into depression. Only one course remained. She had to give Luke up.

Cassie took her suitcase from the rack and started to pack for home. The room had originally been two tiny ones, so that one end was the mirror image of the other. Her toothpaste and hairbrush were in the small washroom on the left; her shower cap and shampoo she retrieved from the room on the right, which was the shower.

After making a final check to see if she had forgotten

anything, Cassie carried her suitcase down the red-carpeted hallway to the elevator. As she rode down to the lobby, she reaffirmed to herself that breaking off her relationship with Luke was the only reasonable thing to do. She would always love him—there was no question of that. But she couldn't spend her life living a lie and pretending he loved her.

Making a decision—any decision—usually lifted Cassie's spirits, but today they plummeted steadily on the drive back to Plymouth. Yet she felt she had made the correct choice. If Luke wanted only her money, a marriage would be doomed to failure from the outset. And he hadn't even had the decency to propose.

Why had she let herself be so taken in? As tears again threatened, Cassie's anger flared in defense. Tears would leave her much too vulnerable. She would be easy prey for her traitorous feelings. But she never cried when she was really mad, so she forced herself to recall every word of their last argument, everything Luke had ever said that would strengthen her resolve.

By the time she reached Plymouth, grim determination had taken over. She was going to end their relationship, and she was going to do it in a way Luke would understand.

Without even taking the time to carry her suitcase to her room, Cassie dialed the Daisy Dilly Flower Shoppe. "Hello, this is Cassie Collins. No, I don't want to speak with Mr. Glass. I have an order to place."

She waited impatiently as the gum-popping manager searched first for a pencil, then for the order pad. "Look in the slot on the shelf beneath the cash register," Cassie finally suggested. "You've got it? Okay, I want you to send a bon-voyage wreath to Luke Bennett at 1212 Navigation, Apartment 419. Roses? No, I have something a little different in mind. Make it out of black tulips. Black. That's right. Yes, I realize that's rather unusual, but this is an unusual occasion. A card? No, that's not necessary. He'll know who sent it."

Cassie gave the girl her address so she could be billed and hung up. At once, doubt threatened to engulf her again and she almost called back to cancel the order, even though she knew she was doing the right thing. Quickly rekindling her anger, her only ally, Cassie squared her shoulders and dragged her suitcase upstairs, the corner bumping on each tread. At the top, Phuzzbott lay sprawled, asleep. He opened one eye, blinked it in greeting and went back to sleep. Cassie stepped over the prone animal and lugged the suitcase into her room. Phuzzbott roused himself from his lethargy to follow her into the bedroom, deposited himself in the middle of her bed and went back to sleep.

The phone's ringing startled Cassie. If Luke was calling, she didn't want to answer. On the other hand, it could be the manager of the flower shop calling to confirm her order. Or Trina or her mother. She wasn't eager to talk to them, either. But maybe it was an emergency. Cassie muttered under her breath. She had never been able to let a phone ring unanswered.

"Hello?" she snapped into the receiver.

"Where in the hell have you been?" Luke's angry voice demanded.

"Good-bye." Cassie hung up.

Again the phone shrilled. This time she answered it with, "Go away."

"I've been trying to call you all weekend. When you weren't home Sunday night I was worried sick. Are you all right?"

"Yes. Good-bye." She pressed the button to disconnect the line, tossed the receiver onto her pillow and headed to the kitchen for a glass of water.

Half an hour later, as she sat at the kitchen table with only her thoughts for company, the front doorbell rang. Cassie glared suspiciously toward the doorway that led to the front of the house. Luke was at work, and neither Trina nor her mother would have come to the front door. The bell sounded again, and with trepidation, Cassie approached the door. Through the peephole she could see a man in a delivery uniform.

She opened the door and looked up to the cloud of balloons he held on strings.

"Cassie Collins?" he asked.

She nodded.

"Balloon delivery." He cleared his throat and read from the card, "Roses are red, daisies are white; I'll make up with you, if it takes all night. Signed: Love, Luke."

"Luke wrote that?"

"I just deliver, ma'am."

"Thanks," she said wryly as he handed her the balloons.

He nodded and went back to his delivery van. Cassie took the bunch of helium-filled balloons inside and tied the string cluster to the stair rail. In her plan to end it with Luke, she had never considered that he might dispute her decision.

Half an hour later, the front bell rang again. Cassie opened it to the same delivery man with another bouquet of balloons.

He looked at her oddly, then produced a card. "Roses are red, daisies—"

"I've heard it."

"This is another delivery."

She frowned but took the balloons. "Obviously, there is some mistake. You've already delivered my balloons."

"No mistake. I guess he wanted to be sure you got the message."

"Thank you again." She closed the door and tied this bunch on the hall tree. Leave it to Luke to make things difficult for her.

Thirty minutes later, the bell rang again. "You're kidding!" Cassie said as she opened the door.

The delivery man just shrugged. "Every time I get back to the store, they send me back here."

"Same message?"

He nodded. "You want to hear it again?"

"No, I get the picture."

She secured this bunch to the filigree of the table lamp. Surely, she thought, this will be the last delivery.

By five o'clock there were balloons in all the downstairs rooms. Everywhere she looked, brightly colored orbs floated and bounced. Rainbow colors, interspersed with shiny aluminum ones, bobbed toward the high ceilings and wafted in the air blown from the heating ducts. And once more the doorbell rang.

"Lady, make up with him," the delivery man pleaded. "I'm wearing out the tires on my van driving from here to the shop and back."

"I told you to stop bringing them. Cancel the order."

"I can't do that. He pays for them; I have to deliver them." He thrust the bundle of strings toward Cassie, then turned and strode away. "See you later," he called over his shoulder.

Cassie fastened the newest arrivals to the knob on the television. Her entire house looked as if it might lift off its foundation on balloon power. "That does it!" she remarked to Phuzzbott, who was blinking up sleepily at the balloons. "I'm going to put a stop to this."

She pulled on her coat as she went out the back door. Luke would be home from work by now, and if she hurried he could call the balloon delivery service and cancel the order before even more came. Cassie drove to Luke's apartment and banged on his door. When he opened it, she stormed, "Turn off the balloons!"

"What's the meaning of *this!*" he demanded at the same time, brandishing the black bon-voyage wreath at her.

"You ought to know exactly what that means! Good-bye. Hit the road. Clear out."

"Get in here," he growled as some of his neighbors strolled by, eyeing them with interest.

Cassie pushed past him. "My whole house looks like Disneyland. Call off the balloons."

"You like balloons."

"I like chocolate, too, but I don't want to swim in it!"

"Might be fun. It sounds pretty kinky." He maddened her further by grinning. "Besides, it worked. You're here and talking to me."

"No, Luke. This is shouting, not talking. And as soon as you call off the balloon man, I'm going to stop shouting *and* talking to you."

"Then I won't call him off." His voice softened as he said, "Where were you the last few days?"

"I went up to Salem." She turned her back on him. When he looked at her like that she couldn't stay firm in her resolve. "I needed to think."

"And you decided not to see me again? I think you need to go over it one more time if that's your decision."

"Why!" she tossed angrily over her shoulder.

"Isn't it obvious? We love each other." He turned her back around to face him. "You can't just throw love away. There's never enough of it to have some to waste."

"Love!" she snorted, trying hard to hang on to her anger. "What about you and Merriweather? Luke, I can't believe you would conspire with that . . . that con man behind my back!"

"Good. I'm glad you can't believe it, because it isn't true. When I figured out what happened, I quit my job."

Cassie stared at him. For the first time she noticed he was wearing jeans and a flannel shirt instead of the suit and tie she had expected. "Quit your job! Why did you do that?"

"I told off that pompous bastard for bothering you and for lying to you about my involvement in his investment plans. Don't look so dismayed. I've already been accepted for another job. International Fabrics Corporation is opening a new branch here. You know, the outfit that's famous for those girdles."

"You're going to design girdles? Oh, Luke, that's terrible! You can't go from space suits to girdles just because of me!"

"Calm down. IFC also makes space suits. In fact, they got the contract with NASA that Pan-Ways wanted." He looked into the dark pools of her eyes. "Why did you leave town without even telling me good-bye?"

When he looked directly at her like that, he seemed so sincere. "I told you, I had to think," she answered sharply.

"At least you could have told me you were leaving. Do you have any idea how worried I've been?"

She shrugged as if he meant nothing to her. She didn't dare speak or she might melt into his arms.

"Damn it, Cassie, you can't run away from every problem. You can't hop a plane and party your way through life!"

"Party! Who said anything about parties? I went to Salem, not Palm Springs. And I drove, I didn't fly." She glared at him. "To hear you talk, you'd think I'm a sequined jet-setter!"

"Well, aren't you?" He returned her frown and his voice rose to meet hers. "Didn't we go on a vacation all the way across the country on a whim? Didn't you take off for Salem without so much as a farewell?"

"Salem is hardly one of the nation's hot spots," she retorted. "And you enjoyed that vacation to California every bit as much as I did! Don't deny it!"

"Yes, I did. But I don't want to marry a social butterfly. I want a wife with a firmer foundation than that. I want the security of a home and a job I enjoy. I like my work. I don't want my wife tooling all over the world on *her* money. I want us to travel on *our* money. Life in the fast lane isn't for me."

"Well, it isn't for me, either. Did we go nightclubbing every night? No, we walked in the sunset and through the woods. Was I dripping in mink and diamonds? No, I wore jeans."

"This time, maybe, but I have it on good authority that there are sunsets on the Riviera and in the mountains of Switzerland. Maybe next week you'll decide to fly over and see them."

"I won't do that!"

"How do I know?"

So it *was* the money, but it wasn't that he liked it more than he liked her. He was saying he'd be happier if she didn't have it at all! Every one of the problems had her wealth at the core. She had lost not only her job but her best friend, and her family was distant to her. Now she was losing Luke over an issue that would never have come up if she still worked for her living.

"Excuse me," she said abruptly. She walked past him to sit on the couch and dug her checkbook out of her purse. "May I have an envelope?" she asked Luke as she wrote out a check.

"What are you doing?"

"May I also have a stamp?"

He took an envelope and a stamp from his desk, and as he handed them to her, he repeated, "What are you doing?"

"Thank you," she replied, not answering his question. She stuffed the check into the envelope, sealed it and stuck the stamp on the upper corner.

As she wrote an address, Luke tried to read upside down. He made out the name of the local cancer research clinic.

Before he could ask any more questions, Cassie stood and walked to the door. "I'll be right back."

Luke watched her cross the parking lot and drop the envelope into the mailbox without hesitation. She came back to him and stood in the open doorway. "There. I just gave the money away." She braced herself for his reaction. If he *was* only after her money, she would soon know for sure.

"You . . ." Luke stared from her to the mailbox. "You gave it away? Just like that?"

"I was happier before I had it. That money was ruining my whole life." Her eyes searched his stunned face. "Will you marry me?" she asked, then held her breath.

"You gave away seven million dollars because you thought it was causing problems between us?"

"It *was* causing problems. Will you marry me?"

"Oh, Cassie." He breathed her name as if he were in shock, but he pulled her to him and held her securely in his embrace. "Cassie, Cassie, of course I'll marry you. I was trying to propose to you before you ran away. But, honey, your money was something we could have worked around."

She exhaled with relief and rubbed her cheek against the softness of his faded flannel shirt. "You really love me? Not my money?"

"Of course I do." His voice was muffled against her hair, and he sounded worried. "But what happens when you have time to think about it? What if you regret giving it all away?"

"Well, actually," Cassie confessed, "I didn't give away all of it. Some I had already spent, and some of it is in unit trust bonds."

"Bonds?" he asked.

"Yes, two million dollars' worth. I can't get that out for another ten years. But," she said hastily, "as soon as I can, I'll give it away, too. I would much rather have you than the money."

"You already have me."

"But look at all the trouble it's caused!"

"Our trouble wasn't caused by the money. It was caused by our not communicating. From now on that's going to change."

"Then you still want to marry me? I think it's only fair to warn you that the interest on that two million amounts to over two hundred thousand dollars a year." She looked up at him anxiously.

"Honey, if we work at it, I'm sure we can keep that money from spoiling our simple pleasures in life." He hugged her happily, and Cassie returned his embrace exuberantly. "Luke," she murmured in his ear, "Do they really have sunsets on the Riviera? Just kidding," she amended hastily. "I love you."

"I love you, too, and one of these days we'll go see if they do."

Luke swooped her up and carried her back into his apartment, kicking the door shut behind them.

CLAIRE
HARRISON

Silhouette Desire

COMING NEXT MONTH

BEYOND LOVE
Ann Major

The day spilled into years and Morgan came after her. Could they pick up the pieces, or would Dinah's insecurity destroy a passion that went beyond love?

THE TENDER STRANGER
Diane Palmer

Eric said he needed freedom, yet he'd married her. He said he hated women, yet he tenderly conquered her heart. Was it possible to meet a soldier of fortune on the battleground of passion and win the war of love?

MOON MADNESS
Freda Vasilos

Jason was still the only man for Sophie, and she was determined to recapture that time of passion — the enchantment of moon madness.

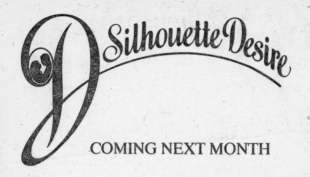